ANDROMEDA

ALSO IN THE RED RAIN SERIES

Red Rain
Project 74
Crook Q
Prisoner 120518
Andromeda
Aurelius
Fox Hunt
Catalyst

ANDROMEDA

RED RAIN #3

RACHEL NEWHOUSE

rachelnewhouse.com

To Thomas
I love you.
I'm sorry.
I forgive you.

JUNE 2076

"Jump, tuck, and roll," they'd said.

It was only after I took a running leap off the moving train that I realized I had no idea how to execute that.

In the split second of panic as I hurled from the train to the building, my muscles did the only thing they could think of. I curled into a ball and threw my hands over my head as the roof rushed up to catch me. My landing was more of a "splay" than a "roll" as I crashed hip-first onto the concrete.

I moaned as the inertia shuddered through my bones. The skin on my right leg screamed, reminding me that the chemical burn I'd sustained this morning was fresh and festering. At least I was wearing thick jeans and long sleeves.

I looked up and was privately gratified to find that my traveling companion hadn't nailed the landing either. Nic stared at his bloody palms and then brushed them off with a wince.

"Can you walk?" he said as he struggled to do the same.

"Yeah." I knew nothing was broken; my hip and thigh would probably just wear a bruise for the next decade. It would go nicely with the leg scars I was no doubt developing under the layers of bandages.

I grasped the ledge and hauled myself up. I glanced over the edge of the roof and nearly vomited. Not because of the height—it was only two stories—but because of the headache that was ramming into my skull like a bull beating down a gate. This was the third time this week that I'd taken a hard impact; it was a wonder I could still remember my name.

I pinched my temples and reminded myself why I had jumped off a moving train. Nic and I had just been deported from the prison island of Rott to be questioned by the United for our various and sundry acts of rebellion—except our train had been "hijacked" by friendly strangers, who, assuming everything was still going to plan, were going to take us to a safe place.

I looked up. Three men were waiting on the roof. They were dressed like maintenance crew, in jackets with a forgettable company logo on the back. If anyone had seen them on the roof prior to our dramatic arrival, I don't think they would have thought anything of it.

I could only hope the passing train had blocked our botched "jump, tuck, and roll" from any nosey passerby.

"Come on," one of the strangers approached me, "we need to get you two out of sight."

He grasped my arm. I was grateful for the guidance; my headache was blurring my sense of direction. He pulled me through the door and down the stairwell to a rear exit, where a windowless white service van was parked in the alley.

Nic followed. "They told me we'd be taking the subway."

"Change of plans." One of them rapped on the rear door of the van. "The subway's been compromised. Our connection didn't make contact. So we're going to have to slog it through rush hour."

The doors opened, and a hand reached out of the shadows in the back of the van. I accepted the offer of help and let the faceless stranger pull me up and guide me into the corner, where I sank down against the wall.

The van rocked as Nic joined us. The doors were slammed and latched without ceremony, plunging us into complete blackness.

"Hang on," an unfamiliar voice said. There was a clatter, and then a weak light flickered on. Our chaperone held a flashlight that cast his features into sharp relief.

I heard the cabin doors shut, and the engine revved to life. The diesel rumble made the whole van shake, and the shudder shot straight up my bones and into my head. I moaned as my headache roared. The whole world swayed, completely out of time with the rocking of the van as it jerked forward. Black spotted my vision.

You're going to pass out. The warning flared across my subconscious. I scooted away from the wall, buried my face in my knees, and closed my eyes. *Breathe. Breathe!* I sucked in a shuddery breath and let it out, then pulled in another. And another.

"Hey. You good?"

Against my better judgment, I lifted my head and looked up. Our escort leaned over me. He'd balanced the flashlight on a nearby crate, projecting its diffused light onto the roof of the van.

"No," I managed, my slurred tone confirming my statement.

"Here, this will help with the nausea." He held out a water bottle—the cap mercifully removed—and a small white pill.

I squinted. "How did you know I was—"

He raised an eyebrow. "You look like death."

I didn't doubt it. I accepted the offerings and gingerly sipped the water. When my stomach didn't refuse it, a took a mouthful and swallowed the pill. Vaguely I wondered where he had gotten it—did they know I had suffered a head injury this morning and came prepared?

Did all that really happen this morning? The day's events flashed through my mind like a movie starring someone else. Nic and I had blown up a factory of dangerous chemicals and released a vicious computer virus onto the internet. We did that.

We destroyed the government's superweapon. We crippled the United.

I repeated that fact over and over in my mind, hoping it would ground me in reality. On one hand, our escapades on Rott seemed like a lifetime ago. On the other hand, my body still felt trapped in that self-destructing factory. I heard the endless sirens wailing, smelled the blood-like stench of Red Rain as it burned through the metal machinery and scalded my leg, and felt myself falling, falling...

"Philadelphia." It was Nic this time. He caught me as I swooned. He took the water bottle from my hand and propped me up against a crate. "Deep breaths."

I ignored the admonition; my lungs were fluttering in tune with my heart. "Tell me what happened. Everything."

His eyebrows shot up. "Why?"

"Just do it! I need someone—anyone—to keep talking." I tipped my head back and sucked small breaths in through my nose.

He shifted uncomfortably. "Umm, okay. Where do you want me to start?"

I used my last remaining ounce of motor control to glare at him. I knew our alliance was loose, but he owed me this one. It was his fault I nearly died in that factory today.

"Okay, okay." He sat down cross-legged next to me. "The United captured us—all of us. You, me—"

"Dad. Ephesus." I wrapped my arms around my knees.

"—and Cea. Yes, that's right." He used the same tone you would with a five-year-old; it seemed to help him as much as it was helping me. "They separated us. I don't know where the others are. They sent us to Rott."

"Ambrose," I growled. My anger gave me a moment of mental clarity. "Ambrose is dead."

"Very much so."

I shuddered, remembering his body splattered on the floor of the burning factory. I tried to muster an emotion—any emotion. Commander Ambrose had overseen the unassimilated concentration camp my family had been detained in, until he'd gotten a better offer to help produce Red Rain. He had breathed down my neck for so long—surely his death should rouse some response from me, Christlike or not. Maybe it was the fog in my head, but I felt nothing, and that terrified me.

"Keep talking."

Nic chewed his lip. "They were making Red Rain on Rott."

"Because my dad finished the formula." That was why they'd chased us down and thrown us in prison: to force my father to finish what Nic had started. Presumably they'd threatened to kill me if he didn't, but I'll never know. My father hadn't explained the last time we talked, before they sentenced me to Rott. He hadn't even said goodbye.

Chaotic emotions came at me in a wave, but they were drowned out by a swell of nausea. Whatever that guy had given me, it was *not* helping. I heaved through my nose.

Nic watched me. "Yes, he did. But we destroyed the factory. We set the systems to overload."

"And you uploaded the virus."

"Nasty bugger," our escort inserted himself into the conversation for the first time. He handed Nic another water bottle. "Where in the world did you get a weapon like that?"

I let my muddled mind churn over the question for a minute. "My brother…" Ephesus had made it, along with a bunch of other programs and prototypes—and it was all on a flash drive that was currently wedged in my shoe. I reached for it.

Nic grasped my wrist. "Less talking, more listening." He pushed me back against the crate, then kept talking before I could muster up the cognitive ability to argue. "The United sent us back to the mainland for questioning, but our friends here intercepted us." He nodded at our escort, who gave a sarcastic salute. "We're going to a safe place, where we'll get our files wiped."

"I have to pick a new name," I whispered, remembering.

"That's right." Nic took a swig of his water and grimaced.

I leaned my head against the crate, questions swirling faster than the stars that were dancing in my vision. I knew it was necessary to avoid prosecution—but how? How could I pick a new name? Not only did I have absolutely *no* idea what I'd call myself, but I couldn't imagine being anyone but Philadelphia Smyrna.

Changing my name seemed like the final betrayal, the last shred of my self-autonomy being ripped from my grasp. Despite all the trauma that had happened to me over the past six years—being labeled a criminal and contained in a camp, having my family torn apart multiple times—my name had stayed with me. I was Philadelphia, and that was something not even the government could take from me.

If I'm not Philadelphia, who am I?

I wanted to cry, but the need to vomit was greater. Before I could register what was happening, I wretched.

"Phil!" Nic dropped his water bottle.

"Everything hurts," I moaned, and I meant it. The feeling of pain in every joint of my body was overwhelming—and so *heavy*. I suddenly felt like I'd left Earth's gravity and was slogging through wet concrete.

"What did you do?" Nic yelled, but the question wasn't directed at me. He grabbed his now-empty water bottle and sniffed it. His voice jumped an octave. *"What did you do?"*

Black again splattered my vision, and this time it wouldn't blink away. I couldn't even see the ground as I plunged.

Someone caught me, but I wasn't sure who. They must have laid me down on the ground, because my body stopped moving, but I couldn't feel anything. Not the van floor shuddering beneath me, not the pain in my joints—nothing. For a brief moment, it was almost peaceful.

The last thing I registered before succumbing to the darkness was Nic screeching.

2

I woke up to silence.

It wasn't a scary silence—the kind where you know there should be sound but there isn't any. Instead, it was an unassuming quiet, like the rest of a predawn morning. The stillness cradled me as I slowly came to consciousness and opened my eyes.

It was dark but not black. Low security lighting near the floor sketched out the shape of a small room. I was lying on a bed in the corner, a blanket pulled tidily up to my shoulders.

I carefully pushed it away, testing my muscles. It didn't take long to register that everything still hurt, especially my head, but the pain wasn't as intense as I remembered. My leg, even though it was still bandaged, no longer burned. I was stiff more than anything, and for the first time in what felt like forever, I wasn't nauseous.

This gave me the confidence to try standing up. I was still in my old clothes—the smell gave that away—but my shoes had been removed. My socked feet touched the cold metal floor, and I panicked.

Ephesus's flash drive! I dropped to the floor and looked around, but it was pointless in the dark. I stumbled to the door and felt the wall until I found the light switch. My eyes protested the sudden brightness and my head started throbbing again, but I ignored the flashing colors and hastily searched the near-empty room.

My shoes were gone. The windowless room contained only a bed, chair, and nightstand, on top of which sat a water bottle.

I picked the water bottle up. The feel of the room-temperature plastic in my hand brought everything rushing back.

They'd drugged us. I'd taken the pill straight like a moron; Nic's water must have been contaminated. Our escort had knocked us out, which meant something was very, very wrong.

I looked at the door. There was no handle, and a piece of scrap metal had been bolted on the wall where an access panel might have been. In fact, the whole room had an unfinished air, like it had been hastily retrofitted into a cell.

My first instinct was to rage like a caged animal, but I swallowed it back. Whoever put me in here couldn't have gone far. So I tried the only thing I could think of—I knocked on the door.

To my surprise, I heard footsteps outside. There was a beep, and the door slid open, revealing two guards. At least, I assumed they were guards; they were dressed in light combat gear and carried pistols. Both had their guns holstered; I guess they correctly assumed I was in no position to jump them.

One lifted a phone to his mouth. "She's awake."

The other gave me the once-over. "How do you feel? Can you walk?"

The answer to the latter question should have been obvious, so I ignored it. To the former, I responded, "Not terrible. Where am I?"

The first slid his phone back in his pocket. "We can't answer that, but we'll take you to the person who can."

They parted, and I stepped out into the hall, which was somehow even more blindingly lit than the bedroom. I threw up an arm to shield my face.

One of the guards pinched my elbow. "This way."

I let him steer me down the hall. I looked in all directions, trying to see as much of the building as I could. But as my eyes adjusted, I realized there was nothing to look at. The entire hall was a windowless tunnel of metal in both directions, and every door we passed was shut. Most of them were unmarked, and some didn't even have access panels installed yet.

The guards opened a door and ushered me into a wing that looked slightly more civilized. There still weren't any windows, but there was a bench and a few potted plants, plus an abstract painting that might have been called art. All the doors appeared to be finished, with lit access panels to the side and shiny numbers above. The guards walked me to door number 6 and punched the doorbell.

A male voice crackled over the speaker. "Is she with you?"

I tensed. I recognized the voice, my subconscious latching onto it as familiar, but I couldn't put a face with it. What's worse, I couldn't remember if the voice belonged to friend or foe.

Although, based on all the circumstantial evidence, it was probably safe to assume he was a foe.

"Yessir," one of the guards affirmed.

"Bring her in, then go get him."

The door beeped and opened in response to an unspoken command. I took a step in and stopped, and time with me.

He sat in the same commanding pose, behind the same excessive desk, with the same ostentatious array of bookcases and soldiers behind him. If it weren't for the fact that the entire room was made out of shiny metal instead of dark mahogany, I would have sworn we were in the same office he'd interrogated me in a week ago.

It was definitely him. His precise dark hair and piercing eyes were unmistakable; he was the man who had held Cea and me hostage to coerce my father into creating Red Rain. I could only hope he had a better plan this time—better than blackmailing my father while I rotted in a cell.

"You again?" I said after an indeterminate pause. Even I wasn't sure if that was an accusation or genuine question.

He gestured to the chairs in front of his desk for an answer.

I shuffled in, suddenly reminded of my socked feet as soon as they hit the plush carpet.

"Oh, my apologies, I had them cleaned." He fetched my tennis shoes from the floor and set them on the edge of the desk.

I sat down in a chair and picked them up. To his credit, they actually did look clean—but of course my brother's flash drive was no longer inside of them. He didn't mention it, so I decided to follow suit. I knew there wasn't any point.

I shoved my shoes back on. "Do I get your name this time?" I asked.

"Thames." He didn't specify whether that was a first or last.

I stole another glance around the office while I fiddled with my shoelaces. It definitely wasn't the same office, so presumably it wasn't the same building. But we were in a high-rise somewhere; this room actually had windows, and they revealed a setting sun and nondescript cityscape. It wasn't a skyline I recognized, but the telltale glimpses of ocean peeking from between the high rises made me hope we were still on the East Coast.

Thames hadn't said anything, so I decided to initiate the questions. "Where are we?"

"My office."

I glared at him. "How did we get here?"

"Everything that comes—and goes—from Rott passes my desk first. It wasn't difficult to interrupt your 'escape.'"

"The virus didn't scramble your systems?" That had been the ace in our escape plan; the virus was designed to wipe all data from any device it infected. Nic had uploaded it to the internet from Rott, taking out the factory and several government servers with it. I had no idea how far the virus had spread, but it should have given them much bigger problems to worry about than a couple of ragtag criminals.

He looked down his nose at me. "You released a virus, not an EMP. I still got the call that you were being deported."

I wanted to be upset that I'd fallen into his trap again, but instead I just felt oddly annoyed. "Then why not just detain us on Rott? Why wait until we'd jumped off the train?"

He looked equally annoyed. "There were... delays in communication."

I closed my eyes. I hoped our real escort, whoever they were, had seen the danger and run the other way.

I took a steadying breath and released a prayer. *What do we do now, God?*

I looked up at Thames, who was patiently waiting for me to process my emotions. "What do you want?"

He reached for a tablet on the desk at the same time the door opened. Nic came in—much less willingly than I had. The guards ingloriously shoved him into the chair next to me.

He looked ready to spout off, but when he saw Thames and I were already deep in conversation, he opted for a sarcastic, "I see you two have gotten acquainted."

"We go way back," I droned, and didn't elaborate.

"Did he tell you anything?" Nic asked as if we were alone in the room.

"Absolutely nothing."

"I'm about to, if you two will let me get a word in edgewise." Thames flicked his fingers across the tablet screen. "It seems we both have a problem, Philadelphia."

He turned the tablet to face me. Soundless security footage was rolling on the screen. I watched as two blurry figures scuffled on the crumbling catwalk in the self-destructing factory on Rott. They were too far away to be identified, their faces obscured by the mess of pipes and machinery between them and the camera, but my memories supplied the screams and shouts that couldn't be heard. It was Nic and Ambrose, moments before Ambrose plunged to his death.

Suddenly, I darted into view. I fell to my knees below the camera, my bleeding hand stretched helplessly towards the men below. Even as a drop of Red Rain slid down the camera lens and stained the image, you could clearly see the terror burning in my eyes.

"I don't see a problem," I said as I tried to swallow the panic that reflexively shot through my system.

"Despite the chaos your little virus caused on the internet, social media has spread this video like the plague. Between this and the virus, you two have become accomplished and—dare I say it—popular terrorists. You should see the hashtags you have trending."

I hadn't been on social media in six years—thanks to the internet restrictions they enforced in the concentration camps— so I had no idea how trending hashtags worked, but I really didn't care. I was a little perturbed that a video of me had been seen by thousands of strangers, but I didn't see how it posed a problem. If anything, I wanted *more* people to see the damage we'd caused.

"Your point?" I prodded.

"The point is, I have a major act of terrorism and no terrorist group to take credit for it. Do you know how much of a PR nightmare that is?"

I didn't, and if he was trying to bait me into a reaction, he was failing miserably. "How is this my problem?"

Nic, who had been watching the conversation with the observant eyes of a hawk, leaned over to remind me, "He could *make* it your problem."

Thames smiled. I rolled my eyes. I knew he could—he always could. That's all the United had ever done—threaten and manipulate and coerce—and I was tired of it. I was tired of rehearsing the same song and dance and reciting the same lines. I was tired of being their puppet, and I wasn't going to play by their rules anymore.

"If you really need pain to motivate you, I can accommodate," Thames was droning, "but I'd prefer to take the easy route—for both of us. I think if you'll listen to my proposal you'll—"

"I don't care," I cut him off. "I'm not helping you. I'd rather die."

Thames blinked, although I think he was more surprised that I'd interrupted him than alarmed at the content of my outburst.

After a beat, he flicked his hand at the window. "Be my guest." Then he leaned back, all his facial muscles relaxing as if he were grateful for the break.

I glanced at the darkening skyline that punctuated the view out his—very high—office window. I swallowed, almost choking on my bubble of courage and anger as it burst.

What have I done? Oh, Jesus, I—

I heard that tiny voice deep inside of me say, *It's going to be all right.*

Sniffing indignantly—it was the most resolute sound I could muster—I scraped the chair back and marched toward the window.

Nic muttered something under his breath I dared not repeat.

I paused in front of the window and took a deep breath, inhaling a dozen prayers with it. Then I braced my feet, squared my shoulders, and grabbed the bottom of the window pane— only to find that there wasn't one to speak of.

Upon closer inspection, I realized the window had no latches and no frame. The surface was completely smooth, its too-perfect image glowing faintly.

"Would you be a gentleman," I snarled, attempting to save face, "and open the window for me?"

Thames obliged by swiping on his tablet. The image on the monitors—there were three of them spaced out across the wall— changed simultaneously to a chirping woodscape with an unseen brook babbling in the background.

"Well, things just got interesting," Nic mused, although he was looking at me, not the fake windows.

I sulked back to the desk. Thames continued seamlessly. "If you are resolute in your desire to die, a functional window will be provided to you. But while you are waiting, will you at least oblige me by hearing my offer?"

"Sure," I said, gracelessly slumping into the chair.

"Thank you," he said, for the first time condescending to match my sarcasm. "It's quite simple, really. I want you to record a few videos for me, Philadelphia. I want you to stand in front of a camera and take responsibility for these acts of terrorism. Tell them you're the face behind the attack."

I frowned at him. "Don't you already have security footage proving that I did it?"

"That *we* did it," Nic inserted.

"Of course," Thames said benevolently, "but that's not the same as you taking responsibility. I don't know how much you know about terrorism, Philadelphia—"

Nic coughed. "More than she cares to admit."

We collectively ignored him. "—but terrorists typically have an agenda. They have demands. They don't typically blow up a factory and release a mastermind-level virus onto the internet, only to vanish into obscurity."

"Why does it matter?" It was a genuine question. Maybe I truly *didn't* know how terrorism worked, but the math wasn't adding up for me. "Say I record these videos and take credit for it. What good does that do you?"

"It gives us a target to eliminate."

That's it? "So I take responsibility, and then you take me down—all through carefully staged videos, of course—so the government can save face."

"Precisely," Thames admitted without shame.

"And what if I refuse?"

He shrugged. "Then I guess I'll find another window."

There it is. There's the death threat. Even so, he wasn't lying—it *was* simple enough. And yet, it didn't seem like the most efficient solution to the problem. Why pick me when they could use—

"What about me?" Nic voiced my thoughts. "What role do I play in this?"

Thames regarded him. "With all due respect," he said in a tone that conveyed absolutely no respect at all, "you have no role in this, doctor. As far as I'm concerned, this operation doesn't involve you."

Nic huffed. "But it's my weapon!"

"It was your concept, perhaps, but you were woefully unable to complete it. Dr. Smyrna is responsible for making it operational."

I flinched, but there was no denying it.

The pathetic look in Nic's eyes said he couldn't deny it either. "I uploaded the virus..." he whined, mostly to himself, sounding like a kid who had lost a game of king of the hill.

"A representation of the younger Smyrna's coding, I understand."

Nic slouched in his chair.

"If I may be blunt, doctor..."

"Please," I answered for him.

"The only reason you're still alive is that we have observed Miss Philadelphia to be capable of extraordinary feats in defense of her family and friends. And you, through some ironic twist of fate, seem to have found yourself in the latter category."

Nic could not have been any more offended. He was flushing both red and white at the same time, and it would have been comical had I not been equally mortified.

The cruel irony that Nic—who had once imprisoned my brother and caused my family so much pain—was now being used to blackmail me was more than my fragile constitution could bear.

What made it worse was the realization that Thames was right.

"But why me?" I blurted, desperate for a topic change. "If we're awarding points based on scientific achievement, I have even less claim to fame."

Thames smiled, which was not in any way a satisfactory answer to my question.

"If you needed a poster child, couldn't you have grabbed any scruffy-looking nerfherder? Anyone could claim responsibility and say Nic and I worked for them. Aren't there plenty of people you could have bribed with money—or threatened with death, since that's more your style?"

He just kept smiling. I locked eyes with him and repeated slowly and deliberately, *"Why me?"*

"I don't like to be wasteful. You were already a loose end that needed to be tied off. Why recruit someone else when I could make a deal with you and solve both of our problems?"

Even I knew that wasn't a cost-efficient solution. Wouldn't it be so much cleaner to use one of his own? Why was he going to so much effort to negotiate with a petty criminal when he could simply order a guard to stand in front of the camera?

Thames correctly interpreted my silence as skepticism, because he continued. "Besides, I know you, Philadelphia. Everyone has a price, and yours is one I'm willing to pay."

He opened a drawer and pulled out a chunky silver object. He turned it on before sliding it across the desk towards me.

My gasp was involuntary. *My reader.*

But it couldn't be. My reader was corroding at the bottom of the sea where Ambrose had tossed it over the boat. And yet, this device looked incredibly familiar.

Nic helped me put the pieces together. "Is that one of my prototype tablets?"

I snatched it off the desk and opened the main menu. It was—it was the reader Mr. Sardis had given me back when my family had been stationed on Mars under Nic. I could tell because all of my note files were exactly where I left them.

Right under the folder labeled "Bible."

I stared at the precious name, afraid that if I blinked the file would vanish again. My last copy of the Bible had been lost when Ambrose chucked my reader into the sea. A small part of me had been worried I'd never see a Bible again—and I'd certainly never expected a government official to be the one to give it to me. It was an illegal book, after all.

I looked up at Thames, unsure which of my dozen questions to ask first.

"It was in the evidence collected from Wing 74. I thought you might like it returned."

I bit my lip.

He folded his hands tidily on the desk. "My terms are very simple, Philadelphia. Record those videos for me—help me clean up the mess you made on Rott—and you and your friend here can go free. I will wipe your files and replace them with clean identities, and you can start a new life, no questions asked."

I stared at him. He seemed completely sincere, and that was terrifying.

Reality hit me in a rush. "What about my father?"

He hesitated, and I thought I'd called his bluff. "And Ephesus? Cea?" I pressed. "What about them? Do they get to go free? How are you planning on tying off those 'loose ends'?"

He sighed. "I'd be happy to offer your father his freedom, if I knew where he was."

"What?" Nic spoke before I could formulate a thought.

Thames snarled at him. "Turns out the chaos your lovely virus caused in our systems made the perfect cover for a little jailbreak. I have no idea where your families are."

I gaped at him. I was battling too many incongruent emotions to form a coherent facial expression. Should I feel hopeful? Worried? Did I even believe him? Thames had been holding our families when we were deported to Rott—that much I knew. Had they really escaped?

Thames returned his gaze to me. "Trust me, if there's any activity on their files, you'll be the *first* to know."

He made a concerted effort to relax back in his chair. "In the meantime, if you'll play ball with me, you can earn their freedom. Do what I say, Philadelphia, and I'll give your whole family clean files."

"Really," I said, the word flat.

"Really. I can make it so that there's no record of anything—no Red Rain, no virus, no criminal charges, nothing. It will be like the last three years never happened. And," he added with an indulgent smile, "you can keep your Bible."

I tightened my fingers around the reader.

Something wasn't right. It was too easy, too painless. Why would he be willing to offer me my freedom when he could just as easily threaten me into recording these videos and then kill me? And what about my father and Ephesus? It was probably easy enough to sweep me and Cea under the rug—we were little more than collateral damage, in the grand scheme of things. But my father, Ephesus, and Nic had been too involved. There was no way the government would be willing to just release them into the wild, not after they'd collectively created several superweapons.

I didn't trust Thames, not for a minute. It felt like a trap. Worse, it felt like compromise.

I started to push the reader back across the desk, but a hand closed around my wrist.

"Maybe you should give her a day to think about it," Nic said, his eyes on mine.

"Excellent advice." Thames nodded at the guards hovering around the room.

I stared at Nic, trying to translate the unspoken message his eyes were broadcasting. After a minute, I nodded and let go of the reader.

Thames waved his hand. "Keep it. As a gesture of goodwill."

I definitely didn't trust any "gesture of goodwill" from him, but for a Bible, I was willing to risk it. I snatched the reader and clutched it to my chest, half expecting him to take it back.

Two guards approached Nic and me. "They will show you the accommodations," Thames said.

Nic and I stood up together. Thames directed his final words at me. "Please, get some rest. We'll discuss details in the morning."

I didn't gratify him with a goodbye.

3

I assumed Thames was being sarcastic by calling our cells "accommodations," but as it turned out, the arrangements were surprisingly generous. They were certainly the most luxurious prison cells I'd ever seen, and I'd been in quite a few cells recently.

In fact, calling them "cells" seemed disingenuous. In reality, Nic and I had a whole wing to ourselves. The guards ushered us through a large gate—it was labeled "B" from both sides—and told us we could go anywhere we liked beyond it.

Wing B was made up of a wide hall that doubled as a common area, off which were at least a dozen other rooms. On the left were the dorms. I had been assigned to dorm 5, which was at the far end of the hall; Nic was a few doors down in dorm 3. On the right, there were several larger doors that the guards claimed led to a cafeteria, a lounge, a computer lab, and a rec room. At the far end of the hall was another large, presumably locked gate marked "C."

Everything was sparsely furnished. There was no carpet, no cushions, no art on the walls. And yet, it felt minimalist, not harsh, as if the place truly had been designed for human consumption.

"The doors on all the common areas are set to accept you both," one of the guards explained. "But only you can unlock your personal dorms."

I assumed Thames and the guards could also unlock them, but they didn't specify.

"Breakfast will be at 08:00 tomorrow and will be available for half an hour. Don't be late," the other guard admonished, not unkindly.

Then without further ceremony, they excited Gate B and left us alone.

Mechanically, both Nic and I walked to our assigned dorms. He studied the darkened panel next to his door, then chuckled humorlessly. "I should probably warn them that you are notorious for overriding this system."

I flapped my hand over the panel next to my door, and a familiar green circle blinked into existence. These were the experimental locks Nic had developed on his Martian base; they read DNA through the hand instead of requiring a fingerprint or face ID. Thames had the same locks installed in his office building where he'd imprisoned me two weeks ago. I guess when they stole Red Rain they decided to borrow a few of Nic's other inventions, too.

Nic was right; the system was flawed, and I'd been able to exploit it to my advantage before. But unless they'd programmed the doors to accept my father or brother, my DNA wasn't going to help us this time.

I stepped inside my room. "We'll talk in half an hour," Nic called just before my door sealed shut. I locked it and didn't bother to answer.

As soon as the silence settled, all of the emotions I had glazed over during the day came rushing back, demanding to be processed. Shock, grief, fear, anger. Gulping down rage and bile, I leaned my head against the cold door and poured all my conscious effort into taking even breaths. *One step at a time. You can do this. Holy Spirit, I need you.*

Straightening, I turned to face the room and instantly lost my fragile emotional composure.

Mama's purple suitcase lay in the middle of the bed.

Suddenly crying, I ran to it and threw the flap open. A quick inventory showed me that all my belongings were there—everything I'd left behind in my cell when Cea and I had escaped from Thames the first time. I sobbed as I ruffled through the clothes and toiletries. My fingers found Mama's floral skirt and clutched it like a lifeline.

I was so grateful to have my stuff back; this suitcase contained the entirety of my worldly possessions. And yet, the whole situation seemed strangely cruel. *He planned this. Thames knew what he was doing all along. He was ready, and I wasn't.*

I blotted my tears on the skirt. *One step at a time, starting with a shower.* I gathered a few toiletries and stumbled into the bathroom.

The bathroom was small and plain, but it appeared to be fully stocked with everything from toilet paper to shampoo. They weren't the dorky single-use products like you'd get at a hotel, either; everything was name-brand and full-size.

On the counter was a clean towel with a shiny packet on top. I picked it up and examined it. It was conditioner—one of those intensive hair masque treatments labeled "for thin and frizzy hair."

I ran a hand over my lifeless, matted mane. Not only had Thames logically deduced that my scalp hadn't seen the inside of a conditioner bottle in weeks, but he'd made the effort to research what kind of hair I had and buy a (rather expensive) specialty conditioner for it.

A new emotion pervaded my already cluttered subconscious. It was that nauseous sense of unease—a clingy premonition that I was falling right into his trap.

Why? Why would he do this—any of this? Why would he be kind to me when it was fully within his power to shove me around? Why was he working with me at all? I didn't buy his flimsy excuses; I knew full well that it would be much easier for the United to dispose of me and cover up the factory incident with creative media coverage. Keeping me alive was a liability. And the fact that he was making a pretense of being nice to me while doing it made the whole situation even more sinister.

Could I trust kindness from someone who had done so much evil?

One step at a time.

I peeled the bandage off my leg and discovered that the chemical burn I'd sustained in the factory had nearly healed. For the first time since the incident, I paused to admire the damage. A splatter of white wounds ran down my shin, forming a morbid constellation. The skin around them was tight and peeling, but it was no longer oozing, and the pain was nearly gone.

Unfortunately, that also meant we'd been out for several days or more.

Swallowing a nip of panic, I cranked the shower on nearly as hot as it would go, ignoring the sting on my wounded leg. Tearing the conditioner packet open, I slathered it on my hair and let it sit for twice the recommended time. I crouched on the shower floor with the water pounding my back, breathing in lungfuls of steam and repeating the same chaotic prayers over and over.

I emerged from the bathroom to hear someone milking my doorbell. I opened the door and was greeted by a frustrated Nic. His look of anxiety melted into one of annoyance at the sight of my wet hair, but he wisely opted not to complain.

He stepped in without being invited, closing and locking the door in one practiced motion. I opened my mouth to say something but decided I'd been in far more awkward situations over the past week.

He walked to the middle of the rug and looked around. "Where's that tablet he gave you?"

"Why?" I flinched, all of my distrust coming out in one syllable.

He held his hand out.

I took a step back. My reader was, of course, where it always was—in the pouch tied around my waist. I slid my fingers, still wrinkled from the long shower, inside and gripped the cold metal.

He rolled his eyes. "Phil, if we're going to get through this, I need you to grow up fast. If you can trust me enough to blow up a factory and jump off a train, I think you can trust me to touch your phone for thirty seconds."

He was right, of course, and I did trust him, to an extent. I guess just wasn't ready to feel the weight of the empty pouch flopping against my leg again.

I gave it to him with a sigh. He flicked it on and rapidly toggled menus. "What kind of music do you like to listen to?"

"Excuse me?"

"I'm a millennial fan myself—you know, the 00s and 10s."

"Are you serious right now?" I squawked, partly because I had no idea what he was getting at, and partly because I distinctly remembered my grandpa telling me that everything produced after the 1980s was unfit to be heard.

"You got another request? Because otherwise I found a Maroon 5 album on here."

"Here where?"

He held the reader out to me, which I took as a cue to step closer. On the screen was the massive file directory for a music archive. It did appear as though he'd found a Maroon 5 album— whoever they were—but what was important was the text he'd typed in the search bar:

OUR ROOMS ARE BUGGED

"Oh—" I started to say, then caught myself. "Please, anybody but them. My grandfather would be appalled." I took the device from him and toggled menus, looking for anything I recognized. I finally found a band that was from this decade at least—some alternative rock something-or-other Ephesus had listened to in college. I picked a random album and hit play.

Nic visibly swallowed a grimace. He put on a brave face and started bopping his head like he was actually into the beat. He jammed his thumb upwards; I cranked the volume, blasting the chaotic tune as loud as my little handheld device could muster.

"Remind me to never let you be in charge of the radio," Nic said, just loud enough for me to translate him over the music. He took the device and set it on the nightstand; far enough away that he and I could manage a conversation, but presumably still loud enough to garble any audio recording.

"How did you find out our rooms are bugged?" I asked.

"I actually don't know that they are," he admitted, "but I think it's safe to assume this entire wing is bugged. There's probably cameras, too. I'll let you know if I find out exactly where they are."

The thought should have perturbed me, but with a twinge I realized that I didn't have the energy to care. For the last six years, my entire life had been under strict surveillance, to the point where I subconsciously assumed that someone was watching me, in some way, at all times.

When did I stop caring about my personal freedom?

"You need to accept Thames's offer." Nic jerked me back to the present.

"Why?" Through context clues I had reached the conclusion that Nic would probably tell me to do it, but I hadn't yet figured out how it would benefit us. Sure, it might save us some pain and bloodshed, but I hadn't exactly been walking the path of least resistance lately.

Nic didn't waste any words. "I think it's our best chance of finding our families."

I skipped my next breath.

"If he's telling the truth—and I realize that's a big 'if'—then he needs those videos to go viral. He needs *everyone* to see them."

My heart and lungs caught up with reality. "They'll know we're alive."

"If we can teach you how to wear a poker face, we can do more than that—we tell them where we are."

"Do you know where we are?"

The silent beat told me all I needed to know. "Did they knock you out too?" I asked.

"Eyup."

"My leg is nearly healed," I offered. "So I think we were out awhile."

"I agree, which unfortunately means we could be literally anywhere."

I glanced around the bare room. "Judging by the lack of functional windows in this place, I'm guessing they don't want us to know where we are."

He nodded his begrudging consent. "I'll figure it out. The computers in the lab have internet capability, and I know that tablet does. Right now everything is connected to a secure network that just has a bunch of games and books and music on it." He gestured at our makeshift radio.

"Secure?" I repeated. "Is that why it hasn't been affected by the virus?"

"Maybe. Or he's lying about how far the virus spread. If I can hack onto whatever network they're using for their communication, I'll find out."

I rolled Thames's words around in my head, trying to shift out the obvious lies. He could have easily lied about the virus, but what would that have gained him? What did any of this gain him? "Do you think he's telling the truth about the others escaping?"

Nic shrugged. "I don't know why he would lie about that. If he had them in custody, he probably would have led with that. 'Record these videos or I kill your father' would have been a much simpler solution. It's what I would have done."

I glared at him, but I knew he was right.

"If I can hack around the internet block, I'll look up their files and see if they've been updated."

"'If' you can hack it?" I echoed, noting the repetition of the word.

He blinked. "If you have any better ideas, I'm open to them."

"Fine." I took a deep breath, tidying my thoughts like a stack of paper on a desk. "What do I do?"

"Buy me time. I need you to play the terrorist as long as possible. The more videos you record—the longer you're 'on air'—the more time we have to figure out where we are and send a message to Ephesus or Cea. This can't be a one-and-done deal."

I knew exactly what he meant. I had seen a lot of government takedown propaganda in my life—they made us watch it in school so we could see what fury would await us if we stepped out of line. The procedure was always swift and tidy to the point of being comical. They showed as little of the terrorist's work as possible, using clever editing of police footage to make it look like the United had swooped in and rained down justice at the first sign of trouble.

If Thames used that script—only allowing me to record one or two statements before he had me removed—then we wouldn't get anywhere. I had to put out a lot of videos over the span of several weeks.

I really did have to play the terrorist.

"Find out how many videos he's planning, and convince him to double it," Nic was saying.

I nodded. I walked over and picked up my reader, eager to turn the volume down. My head was pounding again, this time for more reasons than one.

Nic mercifully took the cue to leave. He let himself out, then turned in the doorway.

"Thanks," he called.

"For what?" I hesitated with my finger on the volume button.

His expression flickered. "Cea is my sister, too." And then he left.

I killed the music app, then sank down on the bed as silence flooded the room. Nic's comment shuddered through me, a chilly reminder that this wasn't just about me, or even about Nic. Our stunt on Rott had affected hundreds of thousands of people. A million had seen the video of our act of defiance—millions more might see the propaganda I was about to record.

I moaned as the realization hit me. If I agreed to record these videos—if I gave the United their clean and tidy takedown—I would be admitting to the world that I was wrong. I would be reinforcing the message that there was no hope in fighting the United, that the government always won. I would be strengthening the monstrosity I had spent so many years resisting.

I flopped back on the bed, sick and tired all at once. I couldn't do it—I couldn't get caught in the same scripted cycle. I couldn't keep bargaining for life and limb while the United always came out on top, always gained a little more control over my life.

If I agreed to Thames's plan, isn't that what would happen? Wouldn't I go back to being a pawn in a game I couldn't control? Isn't that why I nearly jumped out a window today—because I couldn't go back, not ever?

I pinched my eyes shut. If I was honest with myself, I didn't care about Thames. I didn't care about the surveillance video and I didn't care what the United did with the propaganda. If I refused to do it, they'd just cover up the mess some other way. It really *wasn't* my problem.

But Nic was right. It was our best shot at contacting our families, at least for now. And wouldn't it be worth it if it meant seeing my family again?

My reader squawked in protest. I realized I was crunching buttons with my white-knuckled grip, creating a nonsense request the computer couldn't process. I relaxed my fingers and cleared all windows, then opened the file I loved most in the world.

I didn't know all the answers, but I knew someone who did.

4

I almost missed breakfast the next morning, because for the first time in my life I couldn't decide what to wear.

I was halfway through braiding my hair when it dawned on me that I would be going on TV in a few hours. I knew it probably wouldn't be live, but the idea that other people—possibly millions of them—would be seeing me made me second-guess my wardrobe. What in the world did a teenage terrorist wear?

Despite the fact that I only possessed three complete outfits, it still took me a good thirty minutes to answer that question. I ultimately settled on my well-worn linen skirt, walking boots, and gray jacket. At least this outfit didn't make me look like a secretary or something.

It was only after I walked out the door that I realized I looked exactly the same as I did every other day.

It turns out I needn't have bothered, because as soon as the guards ushered me into Thames's office, he pawned me off on a sharp, black-haired woman wielding a comb and hair dryer.

"This is your stylist," he said by way of introduction.

"Narissa," she clarified, then proceeded to size me up. I returned the favor. I wasn't sure what I expected a professional stylist to look like, but I was somewhat surprised to find that her makeup was subtle and her clothes practical. She was, however, heavily armed: A multi-pocketed black tote lay open at her feet, revealing a meticulously organized array of brushes, creams, and paints.

"This is your terrorist?" Narissa ended our mutual scrutiny to cock a sculpted eyebrow at Thames.

He gestured with his hands. "That's why I hired the best."

"You should have spent your money on a better casting choice." She sighed with palpable disdain. I would have been offended if I didn't completely agree with her.

"Well, for starters, we need to lose the skirt and that braid. You look like you're going to ask me if I've heard of our Lord and Savior Jesus Christ, not usurp the government."

The absurd truth of that made me laugh outright. It was only after the sound left my lips that I realized how long it had been since I'd found something genuinely funny.

My amusement faded when she reached into her bag and pulled out a pair of scissors.

"Is a pixie cut too brash?" she asked Thames. "I feel like going all-out punk is cliché."

Thames was about to respond when I cut him off. "Absolutely not. You are not cutting my hair."

I was impressed by how firm my voice was, and judging by the flick of her eyebrows, Narissa was too. Thames was unaffected. "You really don't have a choice in the matter."

I flinched, but I kept the fear out of my voice as I replied, "Actually, I do."

He waited.

"I don't have to record these videos for you."

"And what do you think happens if you refuse?"

I didn't hesitate. "You owe me a functioning window."

Narissa clicked her tongue in amusement.

Thames didn't rush to reply. I took advantage of the moment of silence to release a quick breath and a prayer. Nic's advice flashed across my consciousness, and I slowly organized his theory into words.

"Look, if you want this to work, it has to be convincing. If people can tell these videos are staged—if they can tell you forced some random prisoner to stand in front of a camera and claim responsibility—no one will believe it. Everyone will know that you're covering something up, and you'll have an even bigger problem on your hands."

Believability had never bothered the United before, but Thames didn't interrupt me, so I kept going.

"People have to really believe that I did it. And that's going to take a lot more than a wardrobe change. You can't just throw some eyeliner on me and expect people to believe I concocted a premeditated plan to blow up a factory."

"*Thank you*," Narissa exclaimed.

"What are you proposing?" Thames asked, straight-faced.

I looked him dead in the eye. "We tell them the truth."

"The truth?" he said, although less incredulously than I expected.

"Yes. I go on air—as myself, no makeup, no theatrics—and tell them what really happened. I tell them the story of the poor 'unassimilated' teenager, who's been imprisoned and abused and separated from her family and just finally had *enough*. I'll tell the world why I really blew up that factory: because I didn't want to be responsible for giving you more firepower."

He shared an involuntary look with Narissa. I plowed ahead. "This will take time. I need to record a dozen videos—at least— and release them over the course of several weeks."

His eyes returned to mine. "That's a big investment for a petty terrorist."

"Petty?" I scoffed, mimicking one of Nic's snorts. "I blew up your factory. I ruined your weapon. I know Red Rain was your big project of the year. I know that virus hit several of your fancy government servers. If that were petty, you would have covered it up already." I threw his own words back at him with as much sass as I could muster. "You said yourself—terrorists don't typically come out of the woodwork, release a mastermind-level virus on the internet, and then vanish into obscurity."

He made a vague gesture of consent.

I straightened, drawing on a confidence I couldn't feel. "You can't have your tidy takedown. Not this time. I've caused far too much chaos to be swept under the rug by a carefully edited video. If you botch this, people are going to know that I did a number to the United you can't cover up and started a rebellion you can't contain."

He leaned back in his chair. "I think you're giving yourself too much credit."

"Am I? Then why are you using me at all?"

The silence was embarrassing, and he knew it.

"People are already wondering how—and why—some Mennonite-looking teenager destroyed a factory and released a deadly virus onto the internet. If this were easy to explain away, you would have done so already. But people aren't buying your press releases and official statements, are they?"

My mind began to connect the unspoken dots. Maybe that was why they were using me, why they were willing to go through all this pomp and circumstance for a couple of videos: I broke the mold, and there was no putting it back together again.

Pride rippled through my nerves and strengthened my voice. "You can't just lump me in with the unusual criminal riffraff. I don't fit your profile. People are asking questions, and that's why you need them to see me on camera. You need me to explain my motives and give you a target to shoot at."

He studied me, eyes holding neither agreement nor fear.

"If you want this to go away, we have to do it right. People will believe it, because it will be the truth. Give me time to sell them on my story—at least two weeks—and then, *and only then*, can you take me down."

He lifted his eyebrows. I added one last layer of security.

"If you want your clean, one-and-done takedown—where I record a statement and you swiftly swing in and oust me—then you'll have to find another actor."

I let the threat incubate in the silence.

I'll never know how Thames would have responded to that, because Narissa answered for him by clacking her scissors together twice. "Well," she chirped, "at least let me trim your dead ends."

*

"You convinced him to do what?"

It was several hours later at lunch, and Narissa and I had finally settled our battle of the wills over how short my hair should be. Unsurprisingly, her definition of "dead ends" was far more generous than mine. We'd finally agreed to take three inches off, and while I still felt like she'd been too excited with the scissors, I had to admit that my hair looked amazing. She'd slathered my scalp with a dozen products and used a curling iron to coax some bounce into my flat locks. For the first time in years, I felt pretty, and I was more than a little miffed that Nic hadn't commented on my haircut yet.

"I convinced him to let me tell the truth," I repeated. I pulled my hair over my shoulder and pointedly ran my fingers through the loose curls. Not that Nic had noticed the last three times I'd done it.

"I don't understand." He jabbed assorted steamed vegetables with his fork. "Why?"

"Why not? It will be more convincing."

He wagged his head. "It makes absolutely no sense for them. It's suicidal."

Now I was miffed for more reasons than one. "It was *your* idea! I was just taking your advice!"

"I told you to buy us time. I didn't tell you to be honest."

I sighed and flopped back in the chair. "You're right, I should have known better. None of your plans involve honesty."

There was a beat of silence. Before I could decide whether or not I should apologize, Nic spoke again. His voice was kinder this time.

"Look at it this way. From what you've told me, you've convinced him to let you go on air and tell your whole life story. Being contained in a camp, forced labor, family separation—the works. Right?"

"Yeah, I think so."

"You've basically convinced him to let you rip the United to shreds on live TV."

I sat up.

"What happens to people like you is not something the United talks about. Concentration camps don't exactly support an aesthetic of tolerance and prosperity. Sending an underage girl to a male prison in the middle of the ocean doesn't make them look like the benevolent, caring parent they pretend to be."

"Does anyone really believe that story, though?"

The look in Nic's eyes could only be described by one word—sad. "Enough of them do." He laid his fork down in the pile of obliterated vegetables. "Look, I don't know how much TV you've watched—"

"As little as possible."

"But the United is a very talented actor. They are professionals at using editing and lies to make any situation look good. They can explain anything away with a few tweaks in vocabulary. By slapping some prepackaged labels on you, they can easily make the concentration camps look like an act of mercy—if you only see the outside."

I nodded. I'd seen it done. Years and years of gaslighting and conditioning had shown me just what expert manipulators the United could be. "So what are you getting at?"

"I'm saying it doesn't make sense for Thames to let you go online and air the United's dirty laundry. Your story is not one they want told."

I chewed that thought and a piece of chicken. "Are you sure convincing the internet that I'm telling the truth isn't the bigger problem?"

"I doubt it. They don't tend to concern themselves with pedestrian issues like truth. Like you said—there's no reason they can't just fake a video and sweep this under the rug. That's what they usually do. Besides, airing your story will create more problems than it will solve. At the very least, it's going to get some feminists riled up."

I wanted to laugh, but I suddenly realized the situation wasn't funny. The sense of unease that I'd been harboring returned to my stomach like a stale biscuit. *Something's not right. It shouldn't be this easy.* I tried to swallow the feeling with my bite of food and only barely succeeded.

"So what should I do?" I asked after I'd calmed my stomach with a gulp of water.

Nic shrugged. "If he's going to let you talk, do it. Just don't be surprised if he offers a lot of 'creative direction.'"

"Do you think he's planning on editing the footage?"

"You can only fix so much in post."

The wave of confidence I'd been riding crashed into the shore. I thought I'd cornered Thames, called a little of his bluff. But Nic reminded me that we still knew absolutely nothing. I had no idea what Thames was planning.

And until I found out, I might be playing right into his hand.

5

The fact that the sign was red made me stop and stare at it. So much of my life had been controlled by red signs—usually accompanied by a screech of denial—that it seemed ominously ironic that this red sign had been installed specially for me.

Thames had spared no expense on the recording studio. For some reason, I had expected to record my videos sitting in front of a laptop with some headphones—like most teenagers record videos. But Thames had procured a behemoth of a camera that looked like it cost more than a small car. It hung on a sleek robotic arm, wires snaking up to the ceiling. The elongated lens stared condescendingly down at the room.

In its line of sight was a plain metal chair. Behind that, a frame draped with a huge sheet of obnoxiously green fabric. The whole place was bleached with white light from the dozen lamps crammed into every corner.

Suddenly, I was very glad I had been assigned a stylist.

Thames was in the control booth, visible through a plexiglass window. Servers, soundboards, and monitors crowded the room, barely leaving enough space for the man himself as he hunched over a keyboard.

"Have a seat, Philadelphia," he said, his voice coming from some invisible speaker.

I did as I was told, sitting up straight with my feet flat on the floor.

Thames cast a side glance at me while he fiddled with the sliders on a soundboard. "You're not being interrogated."

"Coulda fooled me," I muttered under my breath.

"Relax," came the repeated admonition.

I sighed and tried to rearrange myself. After a few awkward attempts, I settled on crossing one leg over my knee and folding my hands in my lap.

"Better." He flicked a switch, and the playback monitor above the camera blinked to life. I couldn't help but jump when I saw myself reflected on the viewscreen.

I looked good, I had to admit. Narissa's fawning had done its job; with a curling iron and concealer, she had smoothed over my imperfections and made me look far more put together than I felt.

"All right, before we begin..." I looked up to see Thames scrolling on a tablet. "There are some rules."

I didn't bother to conceal my eyeroll. *Here we go with the 'creative direction.'*

"I want you to start by introducing yourself. Tell them your name, your age, and that you're here to share your story."

Well, that's easy enough. "Okay."

"As you're describing the events, do not name anyone else by name. Do not give any specific locations. Refer to everything in the generic."

"What?"

He kept reading. "You should not name anyone by name—including Ambrose, myself, Dr. Nic, and Cea—or give any locations. Do not tell them you were sent to Mars; simply say you were on 'a research base.' Don't call it 'Red Rain'; call it 'the weapon.'"

"Let me get this straight." My tone was laced with enough incredulity to kill a cow. "You want me to explain to the internet how I got involved with Red Rain—including blowing up a factory of it—without actually calling it 'Red Rain.'"

He tossed the tablet on the desk. "Exactly."

"Why?" I spat back.

He looked up and met my gaze. "If you want me to give your family clean files, you'll do as I say."

I glowered. That threat was the dictatorial equivalent of "because I said so," and we both knew it.

"Besides," he said in a diplomatic tone that did absolutely nothing to restore the morale in the room, "terrorists don't typically disclose their accomplices and whereabouts on live TV. There is a certain *anonymity* to this art."

I slumped back in the chair, crossing my arms. He wasn't entirely wrong; if I were a real terrorist, I wouldn't want to make it easy for the United to find me. I guess my videos would seem more realistic if I acted like I was still on the run from the officials.

But hang on... "Then why would I tell them my real name?"

He bestowed me with another one of his patronizing frowns. "It's not that hard to ID you from the security footage. Everyone already knows who you are."

He turned back to the monitor, leaving me to drown in the thunderous silence his words created in my head. He was right—you could clearly see my face in the clip, and the internet had spread that video like wildfire. That meant thousands, maybe millions, of strangers knew my name. More importantly, hundreds of government officials knew it, too.

And, according to them, I no doubt *was* a terrorist.

Thames spared me the horror of wallowing in that revelation. "Stop sulking and sit up straight, Philadelphia."

I shakily did as I was told. "Where—where should I start, then?"

"Wherever you want. Remember, it's your job to convince me—the viewer—that you're the one behind the terrorist attack on Rott. So, convince me."

Was that a threat? His voice was so controlled that I couldn't tell.

"You're on in two minutes."

The camera whirred. I looked up to see the robotic arm angling the camera closer to my face. The lens twisted back and forth as it focused on me. My glassy reflection filled the viewfinder, where all the fear and trepidation on my face were projected in unnervingly high definition.

I saw rather than felt sweat bead on my forehead. "Will it be live?"

"I don't think that's wise, do you?"

No, I definitely don't.

I swallowed, but nothing slid down my throat, not even air. All my confusion and annoyance at Thames evaporated as I collided with the reality that I had absolutely *no* idea what I was doing.

How on earth was I supposed to convince millions of strangers that I'd become the center of a war I didn't mean to start?

How even *did* this all get started? Nic had started it, of course, when he summoned Ephesus and then Dad to Mars. But I couldn't just talk about them—if this was going to work, it had to be about me.

As if noticing my discomfort—not that it wasn't blatantly obvious—Thames reached out with a suggestion. "Why don't you talk as if you're explaining it to your father?"

My last memory of my father flashed before my eyes—and it wasn't a pleasant one. "My... dad?" I croaked.

"Of course," Thames soothed. "What would you tell him if he were here?"

The words leapt to my mind before I could consciously produce them.

This is all your fault.

I flinched. How could I explain this to my dad? It was, in a very real way, his fault that I blew up the factory on Rott. I blew up that factory because he'd completed Red Rain. He'd given the United a weapon, and I couldn't live with that. I blew up that factory because I didn't want to be like him.

A weight of complex emotions I couldn't process, let alone swallow, clogged my throat. I shook my head to dissipate the visions of my father, searching instead for a neutral face. I couldn't talk to my dad right now. Who else could I explain this to?

Her name came to me like a comforting hug from a friend. *Cami.* I could talk to Cami.

I almost laughed. Cami had no idea what had happened to me after I'd been taken from camp, and if she ever found out, she would *demand* the full story. I didn't know if I'd ever see her again, but if I did, I would definitely have some explaining to do.

I took a deep breath and crystallized the memory of her face. I imagined her sliding across the bus to sit next to me, pressing her arm to mine and lowering her giggling voice as if we were about to share a great secret. I pictured her brother Aid twisting around and looking over the back of the seat in front of us, pretending to be eavesdropping and knowing we both didn't care if he heard.

A little smile crept to my lips, and with that, I knew I was ready.

I became aware of Thames counting down. "On in three, two, one..."

The *On Air* sign flickered on.

I looked straight into the camera lens.

"My name is Philadelphia Smyrna."

6

"That was too easy."

We were in my room after dinner. This time Nic was using a tablet he'd borrowed from the computer lab as a makeshift radio. He'd picked the music before he'd even knocked on my door, and, much to my surprise, he'd held true to his word and dredged up something from the 00s. Also to my surprise, the artificial music, that was somehow both too-bright and too-brooding all at once, was even worse than the noise Ephesus used to subject me to.

I held my tongue, however, partially because Nic had taken the words right out of my mouth. Once I got started, recording turned out to be way easier than I expected.

I'm not sure how long I rambled. Long enough that Thames had to cut me off and tell me that was "enough for today." I started the story with the day we were forced into a containment camp for refusing to sign the file that said we denied all religious, racial, and national identities. I talked about Mama dying, Ephesus getting sent away and reported dead, and Dad being called to work on a "special project."

I tripped when I recounted how Stanyard and Mira had abandoned their family to live with outsiders. Even though I didn't mention him by name, the memory of Stanyard turning his back on me in the schoolyard intertwined with the memory of him running away down an alley, leaving me to die. The images flickered back and forth like a glitched film, threatening to trap me in a replay of abandonment that would never end.

Thames inadvertently broke the cycle by asking a question and prodding me to continue, and I was able to pick up my sentence and keep going. I had just shared how I was forced to stay behind and be adopted by Mrs. Nolan when he cut me off, which I suppose was as good a cliffhanger as any.

I was surprised at myself, but I was even more surprised that Thames hadn't given me any further direction. He hadn't interfered at all, except to remind me once or twice with a subtle shake of his head to steer clear of proper names. Otherwise, he'd let me talk uninhibited, spewing as many of the United's dirty secrets as I wanted, without even the slightest flicker of emotion on his face.

I had planned to tell Nic that. I'm sure he would have been as surprised as I was, but he didn't seem too interested in asking about my day. Instead, he thrust my reader at me and repeated, "That should *not* have been that easy."

I humored him. "What was too easy?"

"Hacking onto the internet."

My shock rose to match his. "What? You did it already?" I looked down at my reader and toggled to the connections menu.

"Yeah. Didn't even take an hour. I found a couple networks, but 'NCC1701D' was the easiest to hack into."

My reader confirmed his statement. The networks menu showed two options. "Wing B Guest" was the aptly, if not patronizingly, named closed network we were supposed to be on. Nic had disabled that one and switched my reader to the new network, which boasted a pleasantly strong signal.

"What can this network access?"

"Just the United internet. I haven't found any servers or clouds shared on the network yet. I might try some of the other networks to see if I can hack into their communication channels—"

"Wow," I interrupted him, partially because I didn't realize he was still talking.

His eyebrows met his hairline.

I clarified. "I can't remember the last time I was on the 'regular' internet."

His lips twitched, but I don't think it was from amusement. "Just remember, if someone asks you for sensitive information, it's a scam."

If his tone had been any drier, I would have thought he was cracking a joke. As it was, he sounded more serious than anything else.

I opened a blank browser window, mostly just to see if it worked. The choices of unrestricted internet access should have astounded me, but I knew without thinking what I wanted to search for. Unfortunately, it was also the one thing I had no idea how to find.

"Have you looked at our files?"

He nodded slowly, as if he had been waiting for me to ask.

"And?"

"Currently, I can neither confirm nor deny whether or not Thames is telling the truth about our families."

"As per usual," I consented, "but how so?"

"Well, according to their files, they're all still contained at Street 87 camp. Your father, brother, *and* Cea."

A brief shot of illogical hope raged through me, but my conscious mind quickly caught up. "There's no way that's true."

"I agree. Especially when there's no record of your reassignment to Mars."

"I'm sorry, what?" I was surprised my brain used actual words rather than stunned silence to communicate my reaction.

He nodded again, even more slowly. "I don't know what to tell you, but according to the main records, Ephesus never went to Mars, let alone died and came back to life. Your father never went to Mars either, and there's no record of him being involved in any jailbreaks or lab explosions—all of which seem pertinent."

A revolting sense of déjà vu washed over me. Wasn't it only a week or two ago that I'd had this same conversation with someone else?

It's bizarre… It's not like it's confidential. It's like Nic never existed.

I stared at him, as if studying his neglected mustache would help me put the pieces together. "Has your file changed?"

Uninhibited offense burned in his eyes. "No. According to the records, I'm still the governor of Base #9.6.11, which is doing quite swimmingly, not that you care."

That information definitely seemed like something we should both care about.

I can't find anything in the news, not even on the Martian sites, about his arrest. There's nothing linking him to the virus. His file hasn't had any new entries since he was granted governorship of the base.

I jumped to the most obvious explanation. "Are there other, less-public records?"

He twisted his hand in a "maybe, maybe not" gesture. "There could be sealed files. I'll definitely keep looking. But the records I hacked into aren't exactly the kind you can pull at a library. And besides, they made the effort to update *your* file."

He made no attempt to hide the scorn in his voice.

An instinctive shroud of fear fell on my shoulders. "What does it say?"

"Only that you had a perfect academic record and an acceptable compliance rate… until you blew up a factory on an island you weren't supposed to be on."

"I don't follow."

"Me neither," he admitted, and the coyness left his voice. "I don't know what's going on, but there's no record of you going to Mars. Nothing about turning me in." He related that fact with no malice at all. "Nothing about being used as a hostage. Nothing about escaping or being sentenced to Rott. There is literally nothing on your file except your graduation and some pending job applications, until a week ago."

"A week ago," I repeated, the underlying significance of those words not escaping me.

"Yup," he confirmed. "They had us out for six days. We really *could* be anywhere. They must have put us both in a medically induced coma—which is *not* a good sign for your mental health after sustaining multiple brain injuries."

I decided not to dwell on that last part, mostly because there was no space in my conscious thought to even process what that could mean. "So what does it say happened a week ago?"

"You were caught on camera assisting in the destruction of a factory on Rott, and that's propelled you to Public Enemy No.1."

I tried to breathe slowly through my nose and hoped he would keep talking and explain.

He did keep talking, but he didn't explain anything. Instead, the more he revealed, the less sense everything made.

"As soon as that security footage was leaked onto the internet, there's a flurry of activity on your file. All of a sudden, there's a top-level investigation into what was happening on Rott. The big boys are trying to figure out what that factory was making and who was behind it all, and you're their best lead."

I shook my head, as if I could rattle some logic into place. "Wait, they didn't know we were making Red Rain?"

"If they did, they aren't calling it by name."

Thames hadn't wanted me to mention the name "Red Rain" on air—but somehow those facts didn't seem related.

"Let me get this straight," I said, even though I knew things were anything but straight. "According to the public records, the United didn't know what was going on—on Mars, on Rott, any of it—until that video leaked."

He nodded. "Thames is telling the truth about one thing— that video gave them a PR nightmare. I'm just not entirely sure who 'they' are anymore."

"But I thought the United was making Red Rain for themselves."

"I still think that's the case," Nic said. I couldn't gauge the level of confidence in his voice. "The computers on Rott were connected to some top-level government servers, so at least *someone* from the United is involved. Plus, that factory cost millions and would have taken months to build—not exactly rouge rebels making Molotov cocktails in the garage."

He sighed. "The easiest explanation is that the project was top-secret, and when the video got leaked, some departments got their wires crossed. If that's the case, the records should sort themselves out in a few days, they'll get their tidy little social media takedown, and everything will go back to normal."

He sounded like he was trying to convince himself more than anything. It didn't sound like it was working.

I wanted to believe it too. Because if the "easy explanation" wasn't true, the alternative was far worse. If the United wasn't making Red Rain, then who was?

I grasped at our failsafe. "What about the virus? Did it—"

"The virus didn't spread very far," he said without the least bit of concern, "but it still took care of Red Rain."

"How can you be so sure?"

"I'm never sure of anything," he said, and I wondered if he actually lived by that mantra. "But the thing about the Red Rain formula is that it was new data. New data is much easier to erase, because there are fewer copies. And based on how hush-hush this whole project was, I can guarantee you they weren't uploading backups to public databases or sharing the formula in chain emails."

I had to admit that was probably a safe assumption.

"I'm not saying they won't try to reconstruct it, but they have their work cut out for them. I saw what that virus did to those servers. Whoever funded that factory, they won't be rebuilding it anytime soon."

I swallowed a prayer and hoped Nic was right. *Please, God, never again.*

"You should be proud of yourself," Nic huffed. "They're crediting you with the virus, too. It was clear it originated on Rott, so, yet again, they're assuming you're the criminal mastermind here."

He had no idea how much I would have loved to share the blame with him. "Why is my file the only one that's been updated? You were in the video too."

"You can't identify me, though. You're the obvious scapegoat."

It's not that hard to ID you from the security footage. Everyone already knows who you are.

I stared down at my reader, which felt strangely cold in my hands. My cursor still blinked in the empty "search" box.

"Look it up for yourself. I sent you a chat with instructions on how to look up the files."

"You sent me a what now?"

"Unless you want me knocking on your door at all hours of the night…"

I grimaced.

"…I need another way to contact you. So I installed a secure messaging system. Well, semi-secure."

I arched an eyebrow.

He shrugged. "Nothing's perfect. But you have to at least be *trying* if you want to spy on the chat records from this app, and as long as nobody's thinking to look, we should be safe."

He tapped the screen. "This *is* a public network. I'm guessing that's why it was so easy to get onto—it's probably a free wifi connection they didn't realize was in range. But that means anyone with administrative access to the network has the ability to monitor the activity of connected devices. But as long as they don't realize that I've hacked the blocks and connected the reader to this network, they won't be looking. But still, watch what you say."

I nodded and closed the browser window.

"I saved it in one of the folders under 'Users: Philadelphia.' I tried not to make it *too* obvious by putting a shortcut on the homepage, in case anyone else picks up your reader. But you won't have trouble finding it."

He didn't offer any more explanation. He didn't even say goodbye; he just turned to leave, taking the radio with him.

My exhausted consciousness became aware of the idiotic music again. I stifled a headache-induced moan.

He glanced back from the doorway. "I'll find out what's going on. Just keep stalling Thames. As long as possible."

I managed a nod, grateful when the door shut behind him.

7

I never did find the chat app. I spent an hour pawing around the menus on my device, opening every program I came across, and none of them had messaging capabilities. I'm sure it wasn't an actual hour, but with how badly my head hurt, it felt like a torturous eternity. Before long, my eyes started to blur, and I was having trouble concentrating on the file names.

It even felt like the folders kept changing. At first, I was sitting at the foot of my bed, but when my headache got too much to bear, I laid down on the pillow. I held my reader above my head and went back to the main menu, and I could have sworn the file list was longer and in a different order. I skimmed through it and tried to pinpoint exactly what was different, but by that point I could barely read the names of the folders.

I gave up in frustration and closed my eyes, hoping the darkness would relieve some of the pain. I ended up passing out, fully clothed on top of the blankets.

My doorbell woke me up. "Phil!" Someone yelled at me through the speaker. "Phil?" They repeated my name a few more times, long enough for me to process that it was Nic speaking.

I sat up. "What?" I yelled—more like rasped—having no idea if he could hear me or not.

"You're about to miss breakfast," he declared, and, having apparently done his friendly duty, left.

I tried to calculate what time that meant it was and failed. Food didn't sound particularly enticing, but my head still ached dully, and I figured starving myself was not a good way to avoid another migraine.

I stood up. Instantly the weight of the bad night's sleep fell on my aching joints, crushing my mood. I stumbled to the bathroom, took one look at my grotesque appearance, and decided I had zero motivation to fix it. I settled for containing my hair in a bun and changing my shirt for one that was less wrinkled. Narissa would fix the rest later.

I made my way to the cafeteria and found the buffet already swept clean, but someone had made up a plate and left it on the counter for me. Whether it was the cook or Nic I had no idea, but I took it gratefully.

I decided to take advantage of the empty room and linger over my meal, cold or not. After a few bites, I took my reader out of my pouch, opened the Bible folder, and there it was—the messaging app. At least, I assumed it was a messaging app, based on the fact that the icon was a speech bubble.

You won't have trouble finding it.

My annoyance at Nic faded just a little as a small smile tugged on my lips.

I decided to deal with the app later and opened the Bible to the chapter I had been reading last. It was one of my favorites—from the Gospel of Mark—but I didn't get more than a few verses in before I realized I couldn't concentrate.

It wasn't that the passage didn't make sense—I practically had it memorized. It was like my eyes couldn't focus on the words. I would read a sentence, and by the time I got to the next one, I would forget what I had just read. I kept losing my place and having to read simple phrases over and over. It was like the words were getting lost in translation between my eyes and my brain, and after twenty minutes of struggling, the only thing I was sure of was that my headache was back.

It was a relief when a guard interrupted me to take me to Thames. I left my reader in my room, charging.

"You look awful," was how Narissa greeted me when I walked in.

I just nodded. It was too truthful a statement to be offensive.

I sat down on the chair in front of the greenscreen, and she started tugging on my tangles. "Are you sure you want to record today?"

"She needs to." Thames appeared in the control booth. "We need to stream a video daily if we want to keep your numbers up."

Narissa grunted. "I'm gonna need more than concealer to make this work."

Thames lowered his tablet long enough to study me. "Did you not sleep well, Philadelphia?"

Like you care. "I'm fine—I just had a headache."

"How bad was it?"

"It's gone now," I lied. I had no desire to discuss my health with him. "How are—ow—my numbers?" I changed the subject, trying not to complain as the hair on my aching skull was yanked around. It was my fault for not brushing it last night.

"Acceptable," he replied, which really didn't answer the question. "But we need consistent videos over the course of several days to truly garner attention. I want you to keep today's video short—no more than fifteen minutes."

"No problem." We'd be lucky if my headache let me get out a complete sentence.

"I want you to talk about going with your father to the base, finding out your brother worked there, getting lost, and accidentally discovering Wing 74."

"Okay."

"Remember—don't tell them that the base was on Mars. Just say 'it was on the other side of the country.' Call Dr. Nic simply 'the governor.'"

"Fine."

"End when you discover Cea deleted the security footage showing you breaking into Wing 74. That should be enough—"

"Wait, Cea did what?"

He arched an eyebrow. "Don't you remember?"

I remembered watching the tapes with Cea after I'd gotten lost wandering the halls of the base. I remembered her playing dumb about Wing 74. And I *vividly* remembered watching the recordings of Ephesus and the emotions they brought.

And now I remembered the screech the terminal had made when I'd tried to replay the video of me walking into Wing 74.

Error: File not found.

"That was Cea?"

Thames nodded in time with my lagging thoughts.

Of course it was Cea. She'd deleted the record to try and keep Nic from finding out. I'd never put two and two together, but looking back, it made perfect sense.

What didn't make sense was how Thames knew all of that. Come to think of it, he seemed to have a disturbingly detailed knowledge of my movements on Mars, almost like someone had printed out a complete itinerary for him.

"How do you know all this?" I tried to make my voice sound curious, not accusatory.

Narissa told me to look up so she could slather my undereye with concealer, so I couldn't see Thames's expression as he replied, "We have all the records from the base."

They must have kept really good records. It probably didn't take a computer genius to figure out that Cea had deleted the footage; I'm sure there was a log somewhere that proved her credentials had been used to override the file. But to know that she had done it while we were in the viewing room together would have required watching the cameras in that room. To know that we were in the viewing room at all would have required reviewing a ton of security footage to track our movements. I had never told anyone except my father about watching the tapes with Cea, and, by his own admission, Thames hadn't been talking to my father or Cea recently.

Narissa finally stopped touching my eyeballs. I looked over at Thames, but he had gone back to staring at a monitor. If he'd picked up on my suspicion, he didn't seem bothered by it.

I tried to organize my thoughts around the ache in my head. Someone had done their research—and a lot of it. Someone had taken the time to scour the records from Mars and track my movements from the moment I got to the base. That seemed like a herculean effort when my involvement with Wing 74 was, at best, peripheral. If they had tracked my father or brother I would have understood, but why pay so much attention to me?

Clearly, someone was deeply invested in my time on Mars. The question was: Why?

*

Nic had already moved on to dessert by the time I got to the cafeteria for lunch. "How was work?" he quipped without looking up from his tablet.

I ignored the sarcasm in his voice because I was relieved he was finally asking. "Creepy and weird."

He spared me a sideways glance.

I shoveled a spoonful of whatever was on the buffet onto my plate and sat down across from him. "Did you know Cea deleted the video of me breaking into Wing 74?"

He put his tablet down. "I'm going to need some context."

"Remember when I got lost on the base and accidentally broke into Wing 74?"

"The beginning of the end."

"Well, after you found me, Cea and I went to the security room and reviewed the tapes to figure out where I went."

"Smart." It wasn't sarcastic.

"She claimed she didn't know where Wing 74 was—said it was probably unfinished."

He nodded. He didn't seem very interested in my story, but to his credit, he kept his eyes on me.

"Well, after she left me alone, I tried to pull up the video to look at Wing 74 again, but it said the file couldn't be found."

"She deleted it," he surmised.

"I guess so."

"First I'm hearing about it," he answered my original question.

Wherever Thames got the information, it wasn't from Nic. I chewed a bite of the ambiguous pasta I'd slopped on my plate and tried to determine the significance of that. "How did you find out I'd broken into Wing 74?"

"Carnegie told me. And besides, I had backups of all the security footage from Wing 74 on a dedicated server. She would only have deleted the public copy on that terminal."

I twirled the pasta around my fork. Even Ephesus had mentioned seeing the tape of me getting into Wing 74. Clearly, Cea's coverup had done absolutely nothing—which made it all the stranger that Thames knew about it.

I looked up at Nic. "Thames knew Cea had deleted the video. He specifically asked me to talk about it on air."

I could tell by the way his eyes flickered and then darkened that it took Nic only a fraction of a second to reach the same conclusion I did.

"Someone went to a lot of work to analyze my every move while I was on Mars," I declared, even though I didn't want to say it out loud.

"Or they've been watching you from the beginning."

I stared at him with unfiltered horror. I hadn't considered it, but it was a much more realistic explanation. "But who?"

He shrugged and sipped his coffee. "Wasn't me. If I'd kept a closer eye on you, we wouldn't be in this mess."

My mind shifted through possible candidates. "Carnegie—?" I ventured, recalling the ancient ghost of a man that had been Nic's assistant.

Nic stared into his cup for a long moment, his face displaying something close to human emotion. "Carnegie kept impeccable records, but sadly we can't blame this one on him."

"Sadly?" I pressed.

Nic looked up. "They killed him after they busted the base— or rather, he decided it wasn't worth living."

"Oh." I shivered. "I'm sorry." I searched Nic's face, wondering if my sympathy would land.

It didn't. He brushed it off with, "He was close to retirement."

I swallowed. "So… who else could it be?"

Nic bravely held my gaze. "I have absolutely no idea."

My mind scrambled for a plausible villain. The United certainly had the power to monitor me that closely, but they hadn't known about Wing 74 until I'd alerted Commander Ambrose. There would have been no reason to watch me before then—no reason that I knew of, anyway. My file also hadn't been updated, so if one of the higher-ups had flagged me for monitoring, they hadn't made a note of it.

Something told me Thames wasn't the mastermind behind it all, either. He hadn't acted like he knew all this when we'd first met in his office a few weeks ago. He'd asked me a lot of inane questions about my involvement with Red Rain—questions he would have known the answer to if he'd followed my movements on Mars from the beginning.

No, it seemed more likely that Thames was getting his information from someone else. I thought back to the hair conditioner that had been left in my room—all the premeditated, sadistic details that had been planned for my arrival. I was now convinced that someone had been watching me closely for a very long time. But who?

And, more importantly, what did they want with me?

8

After lunch I found myself with a near-forgotten novelty: free time. Nic wandered off, and I, having literally no obligations, decided to explore the rest of Wing B.

Next to the cafeteria was a rec room with a few basic pieces of workout equipment and a ping pong table. Beyond that was a computer lab. It was a small room crowded with two computer terminals and a shelf cluttered with tablets, headphones, and other electronic paraphernalia.

At the end of the hall was the lounge. There were a few relatively comfy-looking chairs facing a TV. A rug softened the floor, and the harsh overhead fluorescents had been replaced by homey lamps.

Intriguingly, there was also a small shelf of physical books in the corner. I walked over and scanned the titles. I recognized most of them as popular releases from the last decade, which meant they were all censored media. Still, I wondered about the kind of person who would waste the luxury of real paper books on two prisoners. I ran my hand along the spines to savor the scratch of paper on my fingers, but none of the titles looked interesting, so I left them be.

Out of curiosity, I tried Gate C to see if it was actually locked. It was. *Worth a shot.*

I retired to my room. Stripping the thin blanket from the bed, I bundled myself on the chair in the corner and took my reader off the charger. I figured now was as good a time as any to try the messaging app. If I was only going to be recording for a half hour a day, I'd have a lot of "free time," and the sooner I could master the internet, the sooner I could be useful.

I fired up the messaging app. The username and password autofilled on the login screen. I read the username Nic had picked for me and almost gagged.

"'peanutp91'?" I muttered, not realizing I had said it aloud. Where did he come up with that? It wasn't even clever.

I logged in. The app was simple enough. The homepage had a search feature and a list of my contacts, of which I had only one—"120518," presumably Nic. The left sidebar held my chat history. I had a dozen unread messages from 120518.

I opened them and saw that Nic had, indeed, left me detailed instructions for how to look up my family's files. A quick skim told me that it involved some creative searching and not a small amount of hacking.

I swallowed a gulp of inadequacy. I had no idea how to do half of what he was asking, and several words were completely foreign to me. Despite the fact that the entire world ran on digital, the internet restrictions at camp had been strict, which meant my computer literacy was limited to emails and designing digital presentations for school.

It didn't help matters that my headache was back—had it ever left?—and the words had begun their slow dance on the screen.

I sent Nic a message.

I NEED HELP WITH THIS

I pondered the words after I hit enter, wondering how he'd react to my neediness. Certain death had made us allies on Rott, but holding my hand while I learned basic computer skills might be going a step too far.

Somewhat to my surprise, he replied almost instantly.

MEET ME IN THE LOUNGE

ARE THERE CAMERAS?

YEAH BUT I FIGURED OUT WHERE THEY ARE

I got up, taking the blanket with me. Nic came out of his dorm and joined me in the lounge, where he wordlessly gestured me towards the chair closest to the TV. I tucked myself into the blanket while he fired up some pedestrian sitcom—something bland enough that we could easily tune it out. I was grateful for the monotony of talking and laugh tracks; it was much gentler on my skull than hard rock.

Nic took the chair next to me. I looked up and realized we were facing away from the room's only security camera, which was rather obviously hanging from the ceiling in the far corner. From this angle, anyone watching wouldn't be able to read our lips or see the screen of my reader.

Nic folded himself into the other chair with a casualness and agility that surprised me. "What do you need help with?"

"Everything," I admitted.

I couldn't tell whether the grimace on his face was one of amusement or annoyance.

"You have to remember, my only experience with the internet is a monitored school computer. I don't know what half these words mean." I held my reader out.

He took it. "It'll just be easier if I do it. Let me—"

"No!"

He stopped mid-keystroke.

"Sorry, I mean, I want to learn. I want you to *show* me how to do it."

Now I could clearly tell he was annoyed. "Phil—"

"Don't tell me we don't have time for that. You got places to be?"

He grunted.

"Look." I took a deep breath and struggled to make my emotions coherent. "I want to be useful. Turning over tables of chemicals and blowing up factories isn't always going to be an option. I need to be able to look this stuff up for myself."

He didn't interrupt.

"I want to learn to program," I confessed. He didn't need to know that, but spelling it out was the only way I could make sense of my own thoughts. "I want to be able to do what Ephesus does. I want to fight back. And if I don't know how to run a simple internet search, how can I learn?"

I'm sure he didn't need the whole sob story, but he didn't disagree with it. "Well," he said after a beat, "I wouldn't call this a 'simple internet search.' It's technically breaking into a government database, just not a very secure one. You can cheat the system by pretending to be an employer doing a background check on a potential candidate, and..."

He paused and rolled his eyes to the ceiling. "Three PhDs, for *this*?"

I smiled.

"Fine," he said with a courage-summoning sigh, "I'll show you." He passed the reader back into my hands. "Start by opening a browser window."

*

It took three tries. Nic walked me through it once. Then I tried and failed twice to repeat the steps on my own. On the third attempt, I succeeded and was rewarded with the database's homepage. I was elated. Nic was simply relieved.

I looked up Ephesus's file. Nic was right; there was absolutely no record of his time on Mars, much less his death and resurrection. Instead, his file said he had been working for some generic company since getting out of college. A quick internet search revealed that company to be fake; Nic knew as soon as I opened their webpage that it was a farce. I could tell this both fascinated and concerned him—why the façade?

"Do you think the United covered up Mars because they wanted to keep Red Rain for themselves?"

Nic shrugged. "What's there to cover up? All they had to do was say my base violated 'regulations,' close it down, and send your family back to camp. No need to lie about it."

I kept reading, hoping to find a clue. The last entry in Ephesus's file was from a mere 12 hours ago. Suddenly, there was a bold warning that Ephesus was wanted as a suspect in the Rott case and his current whereabouts were unknown.

Nic muttered an oath.

My pulse jumped. "What?"

"His prints have been flagged." He gestured to some icons in the sidebar.

"What's that mean?"

"It means they're actively searching for him. If he checks in anywhere—even borrows a library book using face ID—it will alert the officials. Anyone using his ID, his name, or his fingerprints will get flagged." His eyes shifted to my face. "This is new as of this morning. I checked everyone's files yesterday."

I stared back at him. "They saw my video."

"Pull up your father."

My father's file was much longer. I could tell just by skimming the first few entries that he had been labeled as unassimilated long before there was a term for it. I rapidly scrolled to the end, where the same red-bordered message appeared.

We checked Cea and Nic, but their files remained untouched.

Nic stared at the dated mugshot that decorated his file, his finger tapping out the rhythm of his agitated thoughts. "Have you not mentioned me in your videos?"

"Thames told me to just call you 'the governor.' I'm not supposed to mention Cea either."

"But your father and brother?"

It took me a minute to explain that one. I hadn't named my father or brother on the recording—but I had given my real name. I groaned. "No, but they know my real name—it isn't a stretch for them to look up my family."

Guilt flooded my soul as the realization took hold: I did this. Because I aired my life's story online, my father and brother were now wanted men. If I hadn't agreed to record the videos, would they have gotten away?

Did I make the right choice, God?

"Well, one thing's for certain." Nic's sigh interrupted my self-flagellation. "Thames doesn't know where our families are—and apparently the United doesn't either."

I tried to decide if that was a good thing or not.

We both ruminated for several moments. Nic kept scrolling on my reader. I stared at the TV, watching the characters comically bicker over some plot device. I traced their dramatic hand motions with my eyes, feeling the same flurry of activity in my brain. It was right there—the obvious conclusion—but it ignited so many new unknowns that I could hardly see through the smoke.

"He's not with the United," I declared, desperate to bring some order to the chaos.

I turned to find Nic staring at me. "Thames isn't," I clarified.

"If that's true," Nic's voice was cautious but not doubtful, "he's still a very powerful man with an insane amount of resources."

I knew Thames was working with someone who had a creepy knowledge of my time on Mars—someone who, apparently, knew more about me than the government did. "I suppose that's not much better."

"It's not."

I curled into the chair, suddenly exhausted from the weight of unanswered questions. "What should I do?" More fear came out in my voice than I intended. "I mean, should I just keep recording videos? What if I'm right and he's not with the United? What if he's... worse somehow? Should I try and find out who he's working for?"

"I wouldn't push him," Nic replied, also with more fear than he probably intended. "This is the same man that knocked us both out for a week. Until we know more, he's holding all the cards."

I chewed my fingernail.

"On the bright side," Nic said in a tone that wasn't positive at all, "we'll know the minute your family is found. The entire government is searching for them."

"That's... helpful, I guess."

"Not if the United gets them first."

Don't let that happen, God! Protect them! Hide them!

I pulled the blanket around my shoulders. "What do you think they'd do to them?"

"At this point, I have no idea—and I don't think they do either. According to their files, your father and brother are accessories to some weapons plot the government was completely unaware of. My guess is they want information more than their heads." He handed my reader back to me.

It felt heavy in my lap. "And me?" I ventured.

Nic looked down his nose at me with an unreadable expression. "Let's just say, you might be lucky that Thames and the United aren't sharing intel."

I pinched my eyes shut. *What am I going to do, Holy Spirit?*

Nic took that as his cue to leave. I heard the chair creak as he stood up. "We'll keep digging," he said for the dozenth time. I appreciated his use of the plural. "I'll message you later."

"Yeah, about that." I opened the app. "What's the deal with this dumb username?"

He shrugged. "No deal. It's autogenerated. You can change it to anything you like."

That was a relief. I started pawing around in the settings. "Can't I just be Phil?"

"No," he said so coldly that I stopped and looked up at him. His eyes were dark. "You can't. Don't use your real name or any of your nicknames, not if you want to live."

I flinched.

"I mean it, Phil. Don't even type your name in a chat—even to me. There should be absolutely no connection to the name 'Philadelphia Smyrna' with any of your online activity."

He sighed, but if I was hoping for empathy, I didn't get any. If anything, his voice got harder as he continued. "Thames is right. Everyone knows who Philadelphia Smyrna is now. You can't go back. That girl is dead to you. For the love of God, let her die."

And without any encouraging word to bandage the wound, he left, leaving me alone with my tears.

9

I cried for an indeterminate amount of time. I wanted to pray, but any attempt at words melted into chaotic anguish. After a while, I wiped my face and opened my Bible, but I just ended up crying again because for some reason reading still *hurt* and it was confusing and everything was spinning and I had no idea what was going on.

My tears finally dried from exhaustion. I skipped dinner and went straight to bed, hoping tiredness would pull me under before my emotions returned.

Nic had already eaten and gone by the time I made it to breakfast the next morning, which suited me fine. I didn't want to see him. He was right; what he'd said to me yesterday was the truth, and I hated him for it.

I'm not sure why I'd gotten so upset. I knew I was going to have to change my name. But I guess I imagined it would only change on paper. My official file might say something else, but to my friends and family I could still be Phil.

And maybe that was true—a week ago, before Thames forced me to become "famous." Now the collective forces of the

United government were looking for me, and the entire internet knew who I was. Even mentioning my nickname could be a death sentence.

My own name had become a curse to me. Philadelphia Smyrna really did have to die.

And right now, she felt like she was halfway there.

My sour mood—and headache—followed me into the recording studio. I managed to stop crying long enough for Narissa to plaster my face with makeup, but no amount of mascara could conceal how bloodshot my eyes were.

Thames was too engrossed in directing to notice at first. "I'd like to get most of the way through your time on Mars today. Talk about digging for information about your brother, getting a reader with a Bible on it..."

"What?" I grunted.

"The one Mr. Sardis gave you."

I knew what he meant, of course—it was the same reader I had now. When I first came to Mars, I didn't have a Bible, so the kindly horticulturalist had downloaded one from Nic's private server. It was my first indication that Nic wasn't all that he appeared.

"You really want me to talk about that?" My question was genuine, not that you could tell by my tone of voice. I was so used to referring to everything in the generic that I was surprised he wanted me to be explicit about all the illegal media Nic had kept.

"Religion is the lynchpin of your story, is it not?" He finally looked at me. "We're trying to sell them your authentic story, and I think... Is everything all right, Philadelphia?"

I cringed. It was an idiotic question—*You're blackmailing me into recording these videos; everything is definitely* not *all right*—but more bothersome was his use of my name. I loathed how it sounded coming from his lips, and the careless way he tossed it around only added insult to injury. *If I can't use my own name, you can't either!*

I brazenly dismissed his question with a salty, "I'm fine."

"Liar," Narissa hissed in my ear.

I brushed her away. "Stop touching my hair."

Her sculpted eyebrows twitched. She stood back and regarded me for a moment, then obeyed. She dropped her comb into her bag with a contemplative *hmm* and walked away.

"I see," was Thames's only comment. "As I was saying, let's try to get through your reunification with Ephesus, learning about 'the weapon,' and your father's refusal to do the job. I think if you end right when you realize 'the governor' has your father, that will make a great ending, and we can save your improvised escape for tomorrow."

He sounded altogether too chipper about the whole ordeal, like he imagined himself the director of an adventurous TV show. But I was in no mood to argue; I just wanted to get it over with so I could go lie down.

"Sure, whatever," I acknowledged and adjusted my position.

He gave me another sideways glance and started the countdown.

The first half of my stream went, for lack of a better word, "fine." I spoke clearly and coherently, and, with the exception of getting a bit teary-eyed while talking about Ephesus's return, I managed to keep my raw emotions in check. But that was also the problem—there was *no* emotion in my delivery. I droned on in a monotone, gaze wandering anywhere but the camera. In the viewfinder I could see that my eyes were so swollen and bloodshot that I looked drugged.

I could tell by the crease of his lips that Thames wasn't pleased, but he wasn't motivated enough to stop the recording and scold me. He tried various hand motions to get me to be more engaging, but I purposefully ignored them all.

It wasn't until I got to the part about Red Rain that I suddenly remembered I had emotions, and a lot of them.

"I didn't understand exactly what the weapon was," I narrated, "but my brother was insistent that our father not work on it."

I faltered, the competing voices coming back to me.

No! Tell him no! Tell him not to accept. He can't accept.

I remembered Ephesus's panic, the feel of his palms digging into my shoulders as he shook me. I also remembered my own resolution, my calm assurance that I knew who my father was and what he would do.

He won't.

Something hit the back of my throat.

I forced the next sentence out. "Dad… felt the same way."

I won't work on the project. Dead or alive.

My eyes burned. Was I crying again?

"He knew the project would be dangerous in anyone's hands."

Daddy, what happened?

No, my eyes were dry. Dry and on fire.

"He was going to say no. He was going to refuse the project."

I did work on it a little.

I swallowed, but it felt like my throat was cinching shut. Terror filled my lungs, like a panic attack, but deeper, from the furthest reaches of my soul.

"But then…"

Old man, you nearly had it!

Shut up!

"He…"

It was the only way.

My breath was coming hot and fast, but it felt like no air was leaving my lungs on the exhale. With every gasp I was packing my chest tighter and tighter. Full of fear. Full of pain. Full of rage.

Just go. Please. Before you get hurt.

I saw my father's face, his dry and weary eyes gazing into the distance. And then I saw Ephesus, and Nic, and Stanyard, and Ambrose, and every man who had ever betrayed me, abandoned me, lied to me and refused to apologize.

You… wrote the virus.

Nic won't have to use it.

He already did.

The voices heaped on top of each other—lie upon lie, threat upon threat—like endless shovels of sand burying me under and reminding me I wasn't worth believing, worth saving, worth protecting.

Phil, if you don't come now I'll leave you behind!

And through it all my father's last words kept echoing like a wave slapping the shore, wearing my identity down piece by piece like a rock rolled by the river.

Just go.

He never apologized. He never admitted to what he did. He never even said goodbye. And now it was too late.

Just go.

For the first time, I looked dead into the camera.

Thames, oblivious of the impending storm, gestured at me to continue. I spat out the only thing that could justify the emotions clawing at my stomach.

"You betrayed me."

There were the tears again, but they weren't the wet tears of anguish. They were hot and painful, scratching my eyes as I forced them out with all the words I had been hiding for so long.

"This is your fault! All your fault! *You* did this to me!"

I jumped up, shoving the chair out of my way. It toppled backwards into the greenscreen. I heard the stand crash against the wall.

"How could you?" I probably wasn't in frame anymore, but I continued to scream at the camera. "How could you do this to me? You let them win! You let them win!"

I registered that Thames was shouting at me. I looked up to see him pressed against the glass, saying my name over and over, straining to get my attention. Every syllable rammed into my skull, reminding me that everything was out of my control, and I was being played for the fool, and my life was over, and it was all because my father had completed Red Rain.

"Philadelphia! Sit down!"

The curse was out of me before I could stop it. I didn't want to stop it. If I didn't say it, scream it, *do something* to relieve the tension inside of my chest, I knew I would shatter.

"I hate you!"

Thames was silent for a beat—I think because he knew I wasn't yelling at him.

"Philadelphia," he said with a deep breath that fuzzed the intercom. "Sit down. Close your eyes. Breathe."

I ignored all of those admonitions. "I'm not going to do this."

He grabbed a handheld device and smashed a button. "Philadelphia, please…"

"Don't make me do this," I screeched. "Just let me go!"

I stomped to the door. I was surprised that it opened for me; it must not have been locked.

Thames met me on the other side. I tried to shove past him, but he caught my arm. I debated about where to hit him, but before I could react, he grabbed my chin and forced me to look up. He glared at me, but not in a condemning way—it was almost as if he were looking past my eyes, trying to see what was going on behind them.

"Why didn't you tell me you weren't feeling well?" he asked.

I wriggled out of his grasp. "Would you have listened?"

He frowned. "What kind of man do you think I am, Philadelphia?"

The noise I made could most accurately be called a snarl. "Why don't you tell me?"

Nic's warning flashed across my consciousness—*I wouldn't push him*—but at that point I was in so much pain, emotional and physical, that I didn't care. "I know you're not with the United. I know you're lying. Who are you?"

He ignored the question. "Are you still having headaches?"

"Just tell me who you are!"

He had the audacity to shush me. "You need to lie down."

I shrieked in frustration. Filled with utter revulsion for him, I spun away and stormed down the hall. I had no idea where I was going, and I didn't care, as long as it was putting distance between him and me.

"Let me help you, Philadelphia," he called after me, voice temptingly gentle.

"Leave me alone!" I reached the first door down the hall, but before I could see if it would open for me, a gloved hand closed around my wrist. I screamed like I'd been shot and wrenched my warm, but I was rewarded with only pain. The grip didn't give.

A strong arm wrapped around my waist. Someone tall and powerful gripped me to his chest, holding me like you would a rebellious toddler. I fought like one, even though I knew I was hitting only air and body armor.

"Let me go," I cried, more of a moan than a demand.

Thames knelt in front of me. "You're not well."

"Please stop, please stop, just stop..."

"Let me help you," he said again.

I sobbed. "No." *I don't want your help. I don't need your help!*

Thames stood up. "Take her to her room. I'm calling a doctor."

The recessed logical part of my brain acknowledged that was probably a good thing, but adrenaline still burned my nerves, and all I could remember was that he was evil, and I couldn't trust him, and I wasn't safe, and I didn't want him—any of them—to *touch* me.

I shoved, but against what, I couldn't tell. The room was spinning, and my vision was blurry from both tears and a migraine. I collapsed, losing the coordination to do anything but weep.

Let me help you.

The last thing I remembered was feeling very, very alone as big arms picked me up and carried me down the hall.

10

By some miracle, I didn't pass out. I was terrified to think what another blackout would do to my brain, and that fear gave me the motivation to hang onto my last shred of consciousness. I fought through the blinding pain and unstoppable tears to hold onto my self-awareness, narrating what was happening to keep myself grounded in reality.

A guard carried me back to my room. I counted the *whoosh* of each door as we passed through it. He set me on the bed and told me the doctor would be right there. I nodded precisely three times, counting each motion. I took my shoes off—one at a time—and removed my jacket—one sleeve at a time. I laid back mechanically on the pillow and counted off the seconds until I heard the door open again.

The doctor dutifully checked me over, looking in my eyes and throat and taking my pulse, but it didn't take a PhD to know what was wrong with me. I'd banged my head one too many times over the past few weeks, and it wasn't healing.

The doctor sat down in the chair and started typing on a tablet. "Do you know how a concussion works, Miss Smyrna?"

I was still wounded about my overused name, but the fact that he was addressing me so professionally helped me put some distance between reality and my emotions. "No."

"Essentially, the damaged part of your brain isn't getting enough oxygen, so it can't function normally. To compensate, your brain tries to use other pathways to complete the same tasks—it takes the 'scenic route,' so to speak, and that can feel very frustrating."

That's why reading hurts so much. It made me feel a little better to know that it wasn't my fault.

"The trick is to let those parts of your brain rest and then slowly exercise them until they're functioning normally, just like any injured muscle. Your problem is that you're not resting."

I turned my head to see him gazing over the tablet at me. "Talk to Thames about that."

"Oh I will be. In the meantime, you need to limit how much time you're spending on that reader."

My eyes reflexively looked to where the device was charging on my nightstand.

"At this point in your healing, I only want you using screens for twenty minutes at a time, and only two or three times a day."

You mean I can't read? The objection rippled through my body like a pinched nerve. *But my Bible... How many times do I have to go through this?* I closed my eyes.

The doctor kept droning on. "The rest of your day should be spent resting and doing light mental activities."

"Like what?" *What is there to do around here that doesn't involve screens?*

"Do you like to color?" It was said so patronizingly.

"I... don't know. Can't remember the last time I did it."

"Try it. Coloring would be good for you. Or ask that friend of yours to play some easy games with you."

"Nic?" *Of course, who else is there?* "You might have to give him a doctor's order to make him do it."

He chuckled. "I also want you to do about thirty minutes of gentle exercise a day. Slow walking on the treadmill would work."

I sighed, but there was nothing to argue with. I wanted to get better. I *needed* to get better. I didn't want reading to hurt for the rest of my life; the Bible was all I had.

"Okay," I said, opening my eyes to look at him. "And thank you."

He smiled, a genuine gesture. "I'll be sending up some pain medication. Follow the dosages on the side of the bottle. It should minimize the pain. If it doesn't work, or your symptoms change, tell them to call me."

"Yes, sir."

He patted me on the shoulder and left.

As soon as the door shut behind him, I sank back and closed my eyes again. *Now* what was I going to do all day? I couldn't read my Bible, I couldn't watch TV (not that there was anything to watch), and getting Nic to "play games" sounded like torture for both of us. And I definitely hadn't seen any coloring supplies laying around.

What's worse, if I wasn't supposed to be using the computer, I couldn't help Nic. I was back to being a useless victim.

I let out a long breath, hoping the motion would relieve my frustration, but the sound just rasped against my throat. *What do I do now, God?*

About fifteen minutes later, my doorbell chimed. "Yes?" I shouted, hoping they could hear me—because I had no intention of getting up to use the intercom.

The door slid open, and Thames stood there.

I jerked upright, every nerve in my body curling from revulsion. In principle, I knew that Thames was holding me hostage and I had no expectation of privacy. But in practice, I assumed he would have the decency not to violate what very little space I had to call my own.

"Get out," I snarled.

He ignored me and walked over. He reached into the sack he was carrying and removed a white pill bottle. He held it out like a peace offering, and I took the bait. I snatched it from his hand and wrenched the cap off, squinting at the label to see the maximum dosage.

I shook three pills into my hand and swallowed them dry. Out of the corner of my eye, I saw Thames offering me a water bottle. The sight of the clear plastic brought back unwanted memories, but I shoved them away and accepted it.

He sat down on the end of the bed while I chugged half the bottle. "I'm sorry," he said when I came up for air.

"For what?" I could think of a dozen things he should apologize to me for, but somehow I doubted any of those were on his mind.

"You should have gotten medical attention a long time ago."

"You shouldn't have kept me in a drug-induced coma for a week."

"It was necessary."

"I don't think you understand the concept of an apology." I downed the rest of the water.

"You'll understand one day."

"Yeah? When?" I glared at him until he met my eyes. "When are you going to tell me what's really going on? When are you going to start telling me the truth?"

He bravely held my gaze. "Philadelphia, the truth is…"

I steeled myself, prepared for him to tell me anything *but* the truth.

"This is all my fault."

I was so startled by the accuracy of that statement that I was speechless.

"I could have prevented all of this."

A million sarcastic replies leapt to my tongue, but I swallowed them. *Let him talk*, the Holy Spirit admonished me. I used all my willpower to make my voice sound curious instead of angry. "What do you mean?"

His eyes drifted to the wall. "I should have never let you go to Mars."

"*What?*"The confused exclamation ripped out of me before I could filter the emotions attached to it.

"I should have vetoed Dr. Nic's request to have you transferred to Mars with your father. I should have listened to Mrs. Nolan and insisted you stay on Earth. None of this would have happened if you hadn't gone to Mars."

I wanted to hurl. I wanted to scream. And I absolutely wanted to punch him in the face. Memories of Mrs. Nolan's buttery voice and sticky affection weren't helping my self-control in that department, either.

Stay cool, stay cool. It was a disgusting revelation, and it was even more proof that Thames was evil, manipulative, and cruel. Under what circumstances would have it been better for me to be taken from my dad and forcibly adopted by a stranger who hated my religion? But as much as I longed to spit all that in his face, I knew flying into a rage wouldn't get me anywhere. I'd proven that already once today.

Holy Spirit, help me!

"You approved that?" I questioned, after I'd taken a beat to check the temperature of my voice.

He nodded. "All transfer requests from the camps come across my desk."

So that's how you got involved in this. The pieces were starting to snap together, but I needed more. "So you were, like, Commander Ambrose's boss?"

"Regional director, yes."

"And that's your dream job?"

He chuckled dryly. "It pays."

Keep him talking. "So Nic was the one who requested my transfer?"

"Yes, although having met him, I really can't fathom why. He's not much of a family man himself."

I had never stopped to consider why Nic requested me in the first place, and looking back, I suppose it didn't make much sense. It made more sense than whatever warped logic Thames was using to justify his actions, though.

"And you are?" I prodded. "A family man, I mean."

He turned to face me again. "I'm sure this will surprise you, but I actually am. I'm very close to my family."

"Then I don't get it," I said with genuine confusion. "If you're such a big fan of family, why would you want to separate me from my dad? You knew my mom and brother were dead. He was all I had."

"Because," he said without qualm or regret, "you deserved better."

I narrowed my eyes and let him explain.

"You weren't ready for all this... all that. Mars, Wing 74, the politics, the bloodshed. You should never have been involved."

He wasn't wrong, but he also wasn't one to talk. "Then why did you drag me back into it? After we came back from Mars, you could have left my family alone in that camp. You're the one who arrested me to blackmail my father into working on the project. Weren't you?"

Grief pinched his face, but he didn't back down from my stare. "That was not my decision."

I believed him. I was right—Thames *was* working for someone else, someone else who had the final say.

I swallowed. "Then whose decision was it?" *Tell me. Tell me!*

He didn't. "All of this could have been avoided if I had denied Dr. Nic's request in the first place. Mrs. Nolan's application had already been approved—I should have pushed it through. I'm sorry, Philadelphia."

I grasped for words. Utter disgust was competing with my need for the truth. I wanted to show him the door, but I also wanted him to keep talking. I was so close—so close to finding out what was really going on.

Before I could come up with anything, he pulled something else out of the bag and laid it in my lap.

It was a coloring book and a set of colored pencils. I stared at them.

He didn't wait for a reaction. He got up and walked to the door, where he paused and glanced back.

"I'm sorry," he said again. Then, with a sigh that was almost wistful, he added, "When this is all over, I'll do my best to give you a normal life. I promise."

The door shut before I could force anything past the blockage in my throat.

11

I sat on the edge of the bed for a long time, just staring at the colored pencils in my lap. I wanted to chuck them into the wall, to get them as far away from me as possible like they were a ticking bomb about to go off. The colored pencils, the hair conditioner, Mama's suitcase—it was all these little kindnesses and gestures that made me feel threatened and unsafe.

What did Thames really want? I suspected most of what he told me was the truth—at least, it was the truth as he imagined it in his own mind—and that just made his actions all the more confusing and terrifying. He cared about me, or he told himself he did, and yet he was willing to use me and abuse me and ruin my life over and over. Either he was a very sick man, or there was something else going on, something that was bigger than him and his desires.

I suspected it was a combination of both.

One thing I did know for certain: There was someone else behind the curtain. Someone else was involved, and that someone had been the one to blackmail my father into completing Red Rain. They were probably the one with the money—and all the information about my time on Mars. And whoever they were, they must want something more than just a few PR videos. We were in too deep for this to simply be social media damage control. They had an agenda, and until I knew who they were and what they wanted, I would have no idea who my real enemies were.

Just when my grinding thoughts were starting to get painful, my doorbell buzzed again. "What?" I called, tiredly this time.

Nic let himself in.

I sighed. Even though, comparatively, he was the least repulsive person it could have been, I wasn't in the mood for more visitors. "What are you doing here?"

For an answer, he held out a white slip of paper. Even from a distance I could tell it was covered in nearly illegible handwriting—a doctor's note.

I laughed. "I didn't think he would take me seriously."

Nic took the chair across from me and reached for my reader. I didn't stop him. "What happened?"

I tried to decide where to start.

Soft music cued up, then he added, "I saw the stream."

I flinched. "They uploaded that?"

"It was live."

I gaped at him, vacillating between shock and mortification.

He studied me. "I take it he didn't tell you."

I shook my head. *That's why Thames didn't want to interrupt me.* Embarrassment warmed my cheeks. "When did it cut off?"

"Right after 'You betrayed me.'"

I let my breath out, deeply relieved that Thames had been the only one to witness my hysterics.

Nic arched one eyebrow and waited. I rubbed the back of my neck. "I was mad… and had a really bad headache."

His eyes shifted to the pill bottle on the nightstand. "Do they have you on bedrest?"

"Not exactly... but I'm not supposed to be using screens. Guess you're going to have to do all the legwork for now."

"So no reading, huh?" He tapped the screen of my reader.

"Yeah. I guess I'm supposed to color." I tossed the coloring book and pencils towards the end of the bed.

He kept typing and didn't respond. After a minute, I ventured, "Why do you think they're streaming live? That seems risky—if today was any indication."

"They don't have a choice—the United is removing your videos as soon as they're streamed."

"So no one's seeing them?" I felt a chunk of despair drop in my stomach like undigested food. Had I really been wasting all this time and emotional energy for nothing?

"Oh they're seeing them," he assuaged my fears. "You had a good 800,000 viewers on that last one. Going live is helping—it's a lot harder to censor a live video."

"Can I see?" I said, even though I wasn't entirely sure I wanted to watch a recording of myself.

"I'll see if I can find a copy. As soon as the United figured out it was you, they took down the stream. People have been reuploading the recording, but most are getting flagged and taken down within minutes. They probably set up a censorship filter for your face or something."

To think of my face as the object of censorship was both hilarious and utterly dehumanizing. Had Philadelphia become more symbol than person?

"Do you think Thames is the one reposting the video?" I wondered.

"I'm sure he's helping, but most of the uploads are from regular civilians."

I tried to imagine what kind of person would share my videos. Were they other unassimilated? Sympathizers? Were there people out there who cared about what was happening to people like me? How many people like me even were there?

My old camp had been so small, no more than 100 families at its peak, and that had been my entire universe for six years. I had no internet access, and my only connection to the outside had been domineering commanders and belittling schoolteachers. Their mission had been to constantly remind us that we were a dying race, and at some point, somewhere, I had started to believe them.

I realized with some shame that I had never imagined there were thousands—let alone nearly a million—of people like me still out there.

Yet I reserve seven thousand in Israel—all whose knees have not bowed down to Baal and whose mouths have not kissed him...

I registered that Nic was talking. "That's probably why Thames wants you to keep the videos shorter—so they can stream the whole thing before the United has time to catch them and block them. They've been streaming from a different account each time, because the United takes down every account that shares one of your videos."

"Wow," I murmured. I knew this was what we wanted—the entire point of these videos was to cause a stir. And yet, I couldn't help but be mystified that it was actually *working*—as well as be a little bit perturbed that hundreds of strangers were so invested in my story that they'd risk their accounts to share it.

"If we needed more proof that Thames and the United aren't working together, the fact that the government is nuking his videos is decent evidence," Nic mused.

I nodded. "I found out how he got involved in all this. He's a regional director for the unassimilated camps—our transfer requests to Mars had to be approved by him."

Nic knotted his eyebrows together. "How did you find this out? Did he tell you?"

I blushed as I remembered how brazenly I had ignored his advice to "be careful." "Yeah... I kind of blew up at him and demanded an explanation. He gave me half of one."

Nic waited.

"He's basically Ambrose's boss. So I'm guessing that's how he found out about Red Rain—when I reported to Commander Ambrose."

Nic nodded. I slowly put the pieces together in my own mind. "That must be when they decided to keep your research for themselves. But Thames said he wasn't the one who blackmailed my father into completing Red Rain, so someone else is in charge. But he wouldn't say who."

"Unfortunately, until we know who that person is, we really have no idea what we're dealing with."

I replayed all of Thames's words in my head, searching for clues. My mind snagged on the one question I knew Nic could answer.

"Why did you call me to Mars?"

He blinked, caught off-guard by the question.

"Thames said you were the one who requested my transfer."

"Actually, it was Carnegie who recommended it."

I gaped. Carnegie? The frail assistant had hardly given me a second glance the entire time I was on Mars, except to comment on my uncanny ability to bypass security systems.

"He thought it would make your father more compliant if you two were together. He was probably right, but looking back, I see that your father was never the problem. It's always been you."

I took that as a compliment.

The music stopped. Nic stood up and handed my reader back to me. "Here, this should help."

"Help with what?" I picked the reader up and squinted at the screen.

He pulled a pair of earbuds out of his pocket and tossed them in my lap. "Keeping you entertained. I'm not really into games."

I scanned the screen; it was open to my Bible folder. Underneath the text files was a new download—an audiobook.

"Where did you—?"

"I had several saved on my database for Cea. I guess when they scalped my servers they decided to keep my personal library—that's where that music directory came from. I figured it out today because I found some special Eminem recordings I'm pretty sure aren't in the public domain." He shrugged. "Guess you're lucky Thames doesn't seem too concerned with following United censorship laws."

I grinned, feeling the biggest burst of genuine happiness I had in weeks. *Thank you, Jesus.*

I waited until Nic had left before popping the headphones in my ear and relaxing back on the pillow. I picked a book, hit play, and closed my eyes. The lull of the narrator's posh accent pulled me in, and I felt every nerve relax as I absorbed the familiar words without frustration or pain.

I was deep into the Psalms—and probably half asleep—when an obnoxiously loud *bing* shattered my serenity.

I jumped upright. My pulse hit the ceiling and stayed there for several seconds until I realized the sound was coming from my reader.

I looked at the task bar, trying to figure out which program had made the noise. I didn't have any email or social media on this device—what would I be getting notifications from?

Then I remembered—the chat app. Nic must have messaged me.

I opened the program, and sure enough, I had an unread message.

But it wasn't from Nic.

The message—and pending friend request—was from a user named "Aurelius396." There was no profile picture.

A dozen warning bells went off in my head. *No one is supposed to know I'm on here. How did they find me? Who found me?*

I took a deep breath. It was probably just spam. If Thames or someone higher up had found out I'd gotten on the internet, they would have just taken my device away or changed the internet access codes—they wouldn't send me a text. There was literally no one else on planet Earth besides Nic who knew I had this device, so there was no way anyone could find me. It was probably just some creep fishing, or whatever slimy people did on the internet these days.

I should just ignore the message and block the request.

But you should at least read it first... just in case it is something bad. You might need to warn Nic.

My hand hovered over the unread icon. It wouldn't hurt to read it, right? It's not like opening the message would set off a bomb or release a virus or anything. That's not how the internet worked.

I wasn't at all confident that clicking on the message would be harmless, but I did it anyway.

The user had sent two simple words, but those words were enough to send me into a tailspin.

HEY PHIL

12

All of Nic's warnings coursed through me like an alarm.

I mean it, Phil. Don't even type your name in a chat. There should be absolutely no connection to the name 'Philadelphia Smyrna' with any of your online activity.

I could think of no good reason why anyone but Nic would know I was online. That meant this person was very, very dangerous.

What do I do? Don't panic. Stop panicking! Just delete the chat, block the user, and tell Nic. They can't hurt you if you don't respond.

I searched for an "options" menu, the device shaking in my hands. But just when I found the drop-down, typing "dots" appeared at the bottom of the screen.

YOU REALLY NEED TO TURN OFF THE SETTING THAT LETS THE SENDER KNOW YOU'VE READ THEIR MESSAGE

I froze. *Nic! Why didn't you tell me?*

I KNOW YOU'RE ONLINE

I still didn't respond. They didn't give up.

I KNOW IT'S YOU PHIL

Block them. Block them, delete your account, and start over.

YOU'RE THE ONLY PERSON ON THIS NETWORK USING AN EREADER. NO ONE ELSE I KNOW USES AN EREADER LIKE A LAPTOP

I opened the drop-down and found the "block" option. I clicked on it, and a bubble popped up asking me to confirm.
Another message came through.

I KNOW THAMES IS HOLDING YOU HOSTAGE

I hesitated. This person knew about Thames, which meant one of two things. One, they *were* Thames, or were working for him. Or, two, they knew what was going on and might be able to help me.
Was it worth the risk? I was running out of options; Thames wasn't being forthcoming, and Nic hadn't found anything out despite two days of searching.
I typed back.

WHO ARE YOU?

The response was instantaneous.

A FRIEND

That could not have been any more ominous.

HOW DID YOU FIND ME?

THROUGH A FRIEND

YOU'RE NOT DOING YOURSELF ANY FAVORS
HERE

I KNOW I KNOW. UH HANG ON

I waited. About a minute later, they started typing again.

LET ME SAY IT THIS WAY: YOU'RE LUCKY
CEASAR HAS TERRIBLE AIM

Ceasar—that was Cea's codename with the "underground."
This person knew Cea, which was a point in their favor. But what
did they mean about her aim? Cea had shot at a *lot* of people
when we broke out of Thames's office, and most of them she'd
hit. I don't remember her missing anyone except…

Hey, drop that gun!

Jayde. She'd shot at Jayde, my sympathetic guard, and
missed, hitting the wall behind him. Looking back, I'm sure that
had been intentional, all part of the theatrics so that Jayde could
play the double agent and help us escape.

My anxiety dissipated as my mind connected the dots. Jayde
was a friend and a member of the underground. He had worked
for Thames, and assuming nothing had gone terribly wrong in
the meantime, presumably still did. He would know Nic and I
had been captured—and he might know a lot of other useful
things.

Jayde was waiting patiently for me to respond. I took the cue
and didn't use his name in chat.

GLAD YOU'VE RECOVERED. DO YOU KNOW
WHERE WE ARE?

NO.   THAMES'S   RECORD   SAYS   HE
CONTRACTED A VIRUS AND WAS APPROVED
TO WORK FROM HOME. HE HASN'T BEEN
INTO THE OFFICE FOR A WEEK

That confirmed my suspicions—Jayde still worked at Thames's main office, but Thames wasn't there, which meant we were being held somewhere else.

HOW DID YOU KNOW ABOUT THIS NETWORK, THEN?

The dots flickered for a minute while he explained.

THAMES'S GOVERNMENT-ISSUED SPYWARE LETS HIM MONITOR NETWORK ACTIVITY REMOTELY. AFTER I SAW YOUR STREAM, I ASKED AROUND AND WAS TOLD Q HAD BEEN REACHING OUT. ALL I HAD TO DO WAS FIGURE OUT WHAT NETWORK HE WAS ON, PULL IT UP ON THE MONITORING SOFTWARE, AND LOOK AT THE OTHER CONNECTED DEVICES. YOU'RE THE ONLY EREADER WITH RECENT ACTIVITY

Thames did say he was a regional director of containment camps; it didn't surprise me that the United had created some fancy program for spying on their prisoners. And Jayde, as a guard, could easily have access to that program.

It all made sense, which was highly disconcerting. Apparently all Thames had to do to see my online activity was log into an app.

As long as they don't realize that I've hacked the blocks and connected the reader to this network, they won't be looking. But still, watch what you say.

Jayde seemed to make the same inference.

IN CASE YOU'RE WONDERING, NO ONE'S FLAGGED OR PULLED A REPORT ON YOUR DEVICE YET. SO I DON'T THINK THAMES KNOWS

THAT'S THE FIRST GOOD NEWS I'VE HEARD ALL DAY

There was a pause before the dots appeared again.

I'M SORRY PHILLI

I pondered his use of the familiar. Had I ever told Jayde my nicknames? He'd asked about them when we first met.

I NEVER GOT A CHANCE TO SAY THANK YOU

His response was fast—too fast.

DON'T

I struggled to come up with a reply. He spared me the trouble.

LOOK, I'M JUST HERE TO HELP IF I CAN. I'D RATHER NOT WATCH THAMES KILL YOU ON LIVESTREAM IF IT CAN BE AVOIDED

I had to admit that was a mutual interest. Jayde continued.

THE SOONER WE GET YOU OUT OF THERE, THE BETTER. I DON'T KNOW WHAT THAMES IS UP TO, BUT IT CAN'T BE GOOD. WITHOUT YOU AND Q HE'LL HAVE LESS LEVERAGE

FAIR POINT. ANY THEORIES AS TO WHAT THAMES IS UP TO? ANY OFFICE GOSSIP?

NOT A WORD. ANYONE WHO WILL TALK KNOWS NOTHING. WHATEVER IT IS, HE'S KEPT IT COMPLETELY SEPARATE FROM HIS DAY JOB

I was disappointed but not surprised; everything we'd discovered so far led me to believe Thames was doing this under the table, outside of United surveillance. Apparently that meant even most of the people in his own office were in the dark.

TALK ABOUT A SIDE HUSTLE

HA. BUT WHATEVER IT IS—HE'S IN BIG TROUBLE WITH THE HIGHER-UPS FOR IT

A hybrid between fascination and fear gripped me.

HOW SO?

THAT VIRUS YOU GUYS RELEASED? IT HIT SOME MAJOR GOVERNMENT SERVERS

This wasn't news to me; Nic had mentioned that the computer on Rott was synced to some important government databases.

IT'S CLEAR THE VIRUS ORIGINATED ON ROTT—AND SINCE THAMES'S OFFICE WAS CONNECTED TO THE SERVERS ON ROTT...

I felt a rush of gratification.

THE VIRUS HIT THAMES'S OFFICE?

EYUP—AND IT LINKS HIM DIRECTLY TO ROTT WHEN HE HAD NO OFFICIAL REASON TO BE INVOLVED WITH THAT PRISON

The fog in my head began to settle. Thames wasn't supposed to be on Rott anymore than I was. Which could mean only one thing: It must have been *his* factory.

HE'S UNDER A LOT OF SUSPICION RIGHT NOW. THE BIG GUYS ARE LOOKING FOR BLOOD

That was Thames's PR nightmare. The virus tied him to Rott, which meant he had to find another scapegoat. That's why he needed me to take responsibility for the virus—so he could make himself look like the innocent victim of a terrorist attack.

But how was he going to explain away the factory? Someone had to fund that multimillion-dollar endeavor, and no amount of makeup and stage lighting would make anyone believe I was behind it all. My videos only solved half the problem.

For that matter, why was Thames's office synced to major government databases? If he wasn't with the United, wouldn't he have set up a private network for Rott? Were other government officials involved? If so, who?

CAN YOU FIND OUT WHAT OTHER NETWORKS WERE HIT AND WHO WORKS THERE?

WE'RE TRYING, BUT THESE NETWORKS AREN'T EXACTLY EASY TO HACK INTO FROM THE OUTSIDE. I'LL LET YOU KNOW WHAT WE FIND OUT

I drummed my fingers on the back of my reader. I was grateful to have Jayde as an ally, but we still had no idea where we were being held, who Thames worked for, or how deep this corruption ran in the United. But one thing I was confident of: Thames had been making Red Rain for himself. Our terrorist demonstration had caused a stir, and he needed to cover his tracks. But who was he hiding from? And, more importantly, what would happen if he succeeded? What came next in his plan?

Whatever it was, Jayde was right. I didn't want to be a part of it. The sooner Nic and I got out of Thames's clutches, the better.

My headache was starting to return. I'd been on the screen too long, but I needed a plan. Thames was going to expect another video tomorrow—what should I say?

I took another wild swing of hope.

DO YOU KNOW WHERE MY FAMILY IS?

NO. NONE OF THEM HAVE TRIED TO MAKE CONTACT THAT WE KNOW OF

My heart sank into my stomach, even though I hadn't really expected a different answer. I nursed my loneliness while the dots did their slow dance.

THEY WERE BEING HELD BY THAMES WHEN YOU TWO WERE DEPORTED TO ROTT. THAT VIRUS HIT ALL OF THAMES'S NETWORKS, SO WE'RE ASSUMING THEY USED THE CHAOS AS A COVER TO SLIP AWAY. WHEN EVERYTHING CAME BACK ONLINE, THEY WERE GONE, AND THE ENTIRE OFFICE HAS BEEN IN A PANIC EVER SINCE

My chest tightened at the realization: Thames had been in control the entire time. He coerced Nic into working on Red Rain, and then he held me hostage and blackmailed my father into finishing it. We tried to escape, but they caught us and dragged us right back to Thames—who deposited us on Rott without a second thought. All this, and yet Thames was pretending to care about me now?

I swallowed the feeling of disgust that rose up in my throat. There was still one person unaccounted for. I decided to ask, even though I wasn't sure I wanted the answer.

IS AUGUSTINE SAFE?

The pause was long, long enough that I feared the worst.

I HAVEN'T HEARD FROM HIM

I hoped that meant Stanyard had gotten away, not that he'd been captured and quietly disposed of.

I sighed. I had no closure, anywhere. It was like my consciousness was a sweater that had been cut down the middle, all the ends left to unravel and disintegrate.

Jayde's message interrupted my stewing.

I'LL LET YOU KNOW IF I HEAR ANYTHING

THANKS

The screen was blank for a moment while we both debated what to do next. My spine stiffened as I remembered something.

HANG ON

WHAT?

IF THE VIRUS HIT ALL OF THAMES'S NETWORKS, WHY DOES THIS PLACE SEEM TO BE RUNNING SMOOTHLY?

I thought back to all my interactions with computers over the past few days. Except for Thames mentioning it, it didn't seem like this place—wherever this place was—had been affected. Nic's music database was intact, after all.

NO IDEA. BUT I'M CONVINCED YOU'RE NOT ANYWHERE NEAR THAMES'S MAIN OFFICE

That was fast becoming the obvious conclusion.

CAN YOU USE THE SPYWARE TO SEE ALL THE ACTIVITY ON THIS NETWORK?

YEAH. SO FAR THERE'S BEEN NOTHING OF INTEREST. IT'S NOT A BUSY NETWORK—I THINK IT'S MAINLY USED FOR ENTERTAINMENT SYSTEMS. THERE'S A BUNCH OF TVS AND GAME CONSOLES HOOKED TO IT

HOPEFULLY THAT MEANS THEY'RE NOT
LOOKING FOR OUR DEVICES ON IT

HOPEFULLY

I opened the network menu of my reader and considered our options. There was "Wing B Guest," but I doubted there would be anything helpful on there. Nic said he found other networks—maybe they had something.

I shot him a message. While I waited for him to respond, I flopped back on the pillow, eager to relieve some of gravity's pressure. I held my reader above my head—and remembered. While I was looking for the messaging app two nights ago, I could have sworn the file list kept changing. I thought it was my migraine warping reality, but maybe it wasn't. Maybe my reader was picking up another network.

I moved the reader around in a slow circle above my head, watching for another network to appear on the connections menu. When I didn't find any, I got to my knees and held it higher. Still nothing. I scooted to the corner of the bed and put my reader against the far wall, sliding it up and down.

I desperately hoped there weren't cameras in my room. I didn't want Thames to see this, for more reasons than one.

I stretched as far up the wall as I could reach—and there it was. A third network, in addition to NCC1701D and Wing B Guest.

I made a note of the name: ECV197. A message from Nic came through; I clicked on it and found a rather lengthy list of networks. Sinking back down on the bed, I copied it, added the network I found, and sent it to Jayde.

TRY THESE. THEY'RE OTHER NETWORKS IN
RANGE

ON IT

A whisper of peace tried to find room in my crowded consciousness. It felt strangely good to have a plan—to know that someone, anyone, was making progress.

I smiled, but the good feelings were quickly washed away by a flashflood of pain. Was it too soon to take another dose of medication?

I NEED TO GO

I'LL TEXT YOU IF I FIND ANYTHING

THANKS

There was a pause, and I thought we were done. But before I closed the app, he sent one last message:

I'M SORRY PHIL. I REALLY AM

13

In spite of everything that had transpired in the last two hours, I actually obeyed the doctor's orders and rested for most of the day. I silenced and closed the messaging app, then turned the audio Bible back on. Within two chapters I was fast asleep. No one woke me for lunch. I was just coming back to consciousness when Nic rang my doorbell and let me know dinner had been served.

I dragged myself out of bed and took a small plate, enough to wash down another dose of medication. I took a shower, braided my hair, and went back to bed as the painkiller kicked in, pulling me into a dreamless sleep.

Thames woke me up in the morning. Thankfully he had the decency not to come in. He informed me that he wanted me to take the day off from recording and reminded me to do 30 minutes of light exercise, per the doctor's instructions. I mumbled some affirmative through the door, and he mercifully left without another word.

I thought about going back to sleep, but as my self-awareness warmed, I realized that I wasn't tired. For the first time in who knows how long, I felt well-rested. I was still somewhat groggy as I wandered into the cafeteria for breakfast, my joints heavy from the abundant sleep. But the pressure—both emotional and physical—had lifted from my head, raising my spirits with it. I scooped up a generous portion of food and dove in.

Nic voluntarily shared the same table in companionable silence. He scrolled through his tablet as he sipped his coffee. I watched the text flickering across his screen and abruptly remembered what had transpired yesterday.

I pulled my reader out of my pouch and fired up the messaging app. Sure enough, Jayde had sent me consistent updates all night—it looked like he had been working well into the A.M.—about what he had found on the other networks.

I skimmed to the bottom and typed a welcome message.

HEY SORRY, JUST NOW SEEING THIS

The typing dots appeared instantly.

NO PROBLEM. WANT THE SUMMARY?

I glanced at the timestamp on his previous message and compared it to the clock.

DID YOU SLEEP AT ALL?

DID YOU?

YEAH ACTUALLY

GOOD

The dots stopped. When I got tired of waiting, I typed again.

SO WHAT DID YOU FIND?

MOST OF THE NETWORKS ARE USELESS— THERMOSTATS AND AIR PURIFIERS AND WHATNOT. BUT ECV197 IS INTERESTING. I

THINK IT'S AN INTERNAL NETWORK FOR
SOME KIND OF RESEARCH FACILITY

My heart leapt at the sight of the phrase "research facility."
My father and brother had spent so much of their lives in various
research facilities that the thought of being near one was almost
comforting, however irrational that emotion might be.

WHAT MAKES YOU THINK THAT?

THERE'S ALMOST NO OUTBOUND
COMMUNICATION. ALMOST ALL OF THE
ACTIVITY IS STUFF LIKE STATUS REPORTS
AND TEST RESULTS. IT'S ALL GREEK TO ME.
I'LL SEND YOU SCREENSHOTS OF SOME OF
THE DATABASES ON THEIR CLOUD—SEE IF Q
MAKES ANY SENSE OF IT

A few images began to load. I looked up at Nic, who had just
started his second cup of coffee, and realized I had some
explaining to do.

So instead of explaining, I just scrolled back to the beginning
of my message history with Jayde and shoved my reader across
the table at him.

Nic's mouthful of coffee ended up back in his cup (for the
most part). He quickly composed himself and started reading. He
held the screen close to his face so I couldn't see the expression in
his eyes. I continued to eat like normal, trying to put on a good
show for the cameras that were no doubt in the room.

After a few minutes, Nic handed my reader back to me.
"Sorry," he said with no detectable emotion, "I thought I disabled
that feature."

I ran my finger around my plate to catch the last bit of
pancake syrup. "Want to watch some TV after breakfast? I have
the day off."

"Aren't you supposed to be avoiding screens?"

"Just one episode," I begged in a practiced teenager whine.

Ten minutes later, we were again arranged in the lounge with a sitcom providing mundane background nose. Nic folded his legs under him, cradling his third cup of coffee in his lap. He regarded me for a solid minute before initiating conversation.

"Remember when you first got to Mars and I told you to keep your head down?"

My eyes narrowed involuntarily. "Yeah?"

He shrugged and picked my reader up. He clicked on the images Jayde had sent and studied them, his eyebrows nearly meeting in the middle as he squinted at the screen.

I gave him a minute. "Do you recognize any of the files?"

"Yup," he said, and took a morale-boosting chug of coffee. "It looks like a carbon copy of all my work from Mars—which I guarantee you is exactly what it is." He grunted. "I guess they did have a backup."

I swallowed a bubble of fear. "Does he have Red Rain?"

Nic was utterly unalarmed. "No—at least not according to these files. This database is several months out of date. In fact, it looks like it hasn't been updated hardly at all since I was governor—it's probably an old server they dragged out after the virus wiped their other networks."

I collapsed back into the chair, releasing my anxiety in a sigh that was far too dramatic for the situation.

Nic looked up at me. "Thames does not have Red Rain," he said with a confidence I wish I could emulate. "If he did, he wouldn't stoop to all these theatrics. A man with weapons doesn't need to cover his tracks."

I had to admit that was the logical conclusion. Thames was trying to cover up Rott; if he had Red Rain, there would be nothing to cover up.

"However..." It was Nic's turn to sigh. "I hate to break it to you, but if they get your father in the same room with this data, he could reconstruct the formula."

He could... and he would.

I avoided Nic's gaze. "Then I guess it's a good thing he got away."

Nic didn't comment. I eagerly changed the subject. "My friend says there's been new activity—so that means we're close to wherever they're doing their research, close enough to connect to one of their internal networks."

"Which, sadly, tells us absolutely nothing. You can build a lab anywhere. We could even be back on Rott, except I *know* Rott's databases are in shambles right now." He passed my reader back to me. "And, if this is an internal network with minimal outbound communication, I'm not sure how this will help us."

The device sank in my lap like a chunk of lead. "My friend said most of the other networks were useless—thermostats and stuff like that."

Nic swirled his coffee. "I figured as much. Sadly, looking at the activity log for the automated thermostat isn't going to tell us anything, except maybe give us an idea of how hot it is outside."

I nodded ruefully. It was a cruel irony that, in a world where every single device communicated wirelessly, we would be strapped for information. Even the locked doors fencing us in were probably controlled remotely.

An idea shot through my brain. The laugh track on the TV seemed to lag as I tried to capture the thought before it faded.

"Nic," I said slowly, giving my words time to catch up. "Do your door locks run on a wireless network?"

He blinked several times, clearly processing the same thoughts I was. "Yes..." The hope in his voice rose and fell with the inflection on that one word. "But unless they've redesigned them, you can't program a new user over wireless. You have to have the physical disc. It's a safety feature—to prevent exactly what you're thinking about doing."

The door. Yesterday. You didn't have access.

No, but you do. And I'm your sister. By blood.

"I may not have to reprogram them."

He didn't ask for more explanation. He looked at me for a moment, then leaned back in the chair and picked up his coffee.

"If you tap the upper-left corner of the screen and hit 'settings,' you can see what network it's on."

I grabbed my reader and got up to do just that.

"Phil," he called when I reached the doorway. I glanced back.

"Be careful."

14

I left the lounge and strode to Gate C. I reached for the panel, then hesitated with my finger poised over the screen. Would it make a hideous noise when I touched it? Would it trigger an alert and cause the Thames to look at the activity log? Was he watching me right now?

I decided it didn't matter. I steeled my nerves—and my eardrums—and tapped the corner of the screen. Mercifully, the only noise it made was an informative chirp.

Several icons glowed to life, just like Nic had said. I tapped the gear to bring up the settings menu. "Connectivity" was the last option.

I wrote the network name down on my reader and went back to my room. I locked the door for posterity, sat down on the bed, and opened the messaging app.

YOU ONLINE?

There was digital silence for one minute, two, and I began to wonder if Jayde had finally exhausted himself and logged off. For all I knew, he was at work. I had no right to expect he'd be at my beck and call at all hours of the day, but I knew I was onto something. The pressure almost made me desperate enough to try the audio call feature.

Mercifully, he started typing back.

WHAT'S UP?

CAN YOU GET ONTO THIS NETWORK?

I dropped him the name.

I'M SURE I CAN LOOK IT UP ON THE SPYWARE. HACKING INTO IT MIGHT TAKE MORE EFFORT. WHAT IS IT?

THE NETWORK FOR THE DOOR LOCKS

The word he sent back was foul, but spoken with admiration, I'm sure.

GIVE ME AN HOUR

I groaned—out loud, even. I'm sure an hour was an amazing turnaround time for expert hacking work, but it was still an hour I had to lie around and be useless.

Well, not totally useless.

I turned my notification volume up to max, cued up some millennial worship music I'd found in the archive, and paced the room. I chanted the lyrics over and over until my heart rate slowed to match the pace of the song, then slipped into prayer.

I tripped over the rug when the incoming message shattered my concentration.

GOOD NEWS BAD NEWS

I sat back down on the bed.

GOOD NEWS?

I KNOW A BIT ABOUT THE SOFTWARE THAT
CONTROLS THE DOOR LOCKS. I CAN LOOK UP
ALL THE DOORS ON THAT NETWORK

I was happily surprised, but maybe I shouldn't have been.
Jayde was a guard, after all. Managing door access was probably
part of his job.

It occurred to me then that getting arrested and meeting
Jayde might not have been the worst thing that ever happened to
me.

Thank you, Jesus.

Before I could celebrate over text, Jayde continued.

BAD NEWS IS YOU AND Q ARE BOTH
BLACKLISTED

MEANING?

MEANING YOU'VE BEEN SPECIFICALLY
BLOCKED FROM ALL DOORS ON THE
NETWORK. ADDING YOU TO THE WHITELIST
REQUIRES A LEVEL 1 SECURITY OVERRIDE

WHAT LEVEL DO YOU HAVE?

LIKE 4

Ouch. I chewed my lip.

CAN YOU HACK INTO LEVEL 1?

I'M SURE SOMEONE COULD

I knew the lack of further explanation meant we'd have to
recruit help—and there was no telling how long that would take,
if we could even find someone to do it.

But, if my theory was correct, maybe we didn't have to add
me to the whitelist.

HOW HARD IS IT TO ADD SOMEONE TO THE WHITELIST?

I TOLD YOU—YOU'VE BEEN BLACKLISTED. I CAN'T JUST COPY AND PASTE YOU IN

I know, I know! Work with me!

OKAY BUT LIKE WHAT ABOUT A NEW USER?

BASICALLY IMPOSSIBLE. YOU HAVE TO HAVE THEIR DNA ON FILE, AND FOR THAT YOU NEED THE PROGRAMMING DISC. WE'VE YET TO FIGURE OUT HOW TO HACK THE SYSTEM REMOTELY

That's what Nic had said, but I knew there had to be a way around it. I kept mashing the idea around in my head like modeling clay, trying to force it into a useful shape.

WHAT IF YOU ALREADY HAD THEIR DNA ON FILE?

IT NEEDS TO BE IN A SPECIAL ENCRYPTED FORMAT—AND NO, I DON'T KNOW HOW TO FORGE THAT EITHER

I KNOW! BUT *IF* YOU HAD THE ENCRYPTED FILE FOR A USER, HOW HARD IS IT TO ADD THEM TO THE WHITELIST?

The typing dots cycled for a minute. I clutched my reader, begging God to help us out on this one.

OH THAT'S EASY. I CAN JUST PASTE THEM IN—IF THEY HAVEN'T ALREADY BEEN BLACKLISTED

I squealed, more to relieve internal tension than anything else. It was so simple; if we could get a copy of my father's or brother's file, we could add them to the door. And, assuming Nic hadn't spent any of his jail time improving the software, the glitch still might let me through.

But where were we going to get a copy of their files? When was the last time they were in a building that was controlled by the DNA locks?

It looks like a carbon copy of all my work from Mars—which I guarantee you is exactly what it is.

Idiotic typos peppered my text as I struggled to type fast enough.

THE DATABASE FORM THE ECV NTWORK ARE THEIR DOOR LOCK RECORDS

He took a beat to translate that. It was a stretch—or was it? Ephesus's prints had definitely been on file in Wing 74. He'd been heavily involved in the creation of that research and had access to all the labs and computer terminals. But were the user files for the doors on the database that Thames had? Had that information been saved? If Thames had literally "copied and pasted" all the data from Mars, it just might be there.

WHO SHOULD I BE LOOKING FOR?

I figured at this point using real names was the least of my concerns.

EPHESUS

HOW'S HE GOING TO HELP?

I flexed my fingers to relax them, slowing my typing pace to a legible speed.

ON MARS, I COULD GET INTO ROOMS THAT WERE SET TO ACCEPT MY FATHER OR BROTHER, EVEN IF I HADN'T BEEN WHITELISTED. I THINK IT HAD TO DO WITH

US BEING BLOOD RELATIVES AND OUR DNA
BEING SIMILAR

His delayed response confirmed I was on to something

SOUNDS LIKE THEY NEED BETTER SCANNERS

LET'S HOPE THEY'VE BEEN TOO BUSY TO
UPGRADE

LET ME LOOK

I flopped back on the bed and closed my eyes. I took artificially even breaths—in and out, in and out—swallowing a plead with each inhale and releasing a thanks with each exhale. Within ten minutes Jayde responded.

GOT EPHESUS AND YOUR FATHER

I cheered into the empty room.

CAN YOU ADD THEM?

I TRIED

AND?

IT WON'T LET ME

My spirit and soul crashed to the floor.

WHAT? WHY? WERE THEY BLACKLISTED?

NO

I scrambled for an explanation, but before I could type anything out, Jayde clarified.

THEY WERE ALREADY IN THE SYSTEM

For a minute, the only movement was my cursor blinking. I certainly wasn't breathing.

Jayde didn't wait for me to formulate words, much less muster the coordination to type them.

THEY'RE ALREADY ON FILE FOR THAT WING. I'D JUST HAVE TO ADD THEM TO SPECIFIC DOORS

That should have been good news, but somehow I knew that it wasn't.

I typed and deleted several messages, struggling to clear away the smoke. Why would Thames already have Dad and Ephesus on file? He didn't know where they were, so it made no sense for him to program them into the system. Unless…

I felt sick just typing the words.

DO YOU THINK HE'S EXPECTING THEM TO COME HERE?

It was plausible, all too plausible. I thought of all the planning and preparation Thames had done to bring Nic and me here and realized nothing was out of his reach. Was he looking for Dad and Ephesus too? Was he lying about giving us all clean files? Was he planning on keeping us all imprisoned here? For what? What if—

Jayde derailed my panic train.

NO I MEAN IT'S LIKE THEY *WERE* HERE. THERE'S ACTIVITY LOGS UNDER BOTH OF THEIR NAMES FOR SEVERAL DOORS ON THIS NETWORK

Hope strangled me. *It can't be. Could they? Are they?*

WHEN WAS THE LAST ENTRY?

ABOUT SIX MONTHS AGO

I did the math. That was when we were all on—

My head spun, but for once, it wasn't because I was getting a migraine.

I scrambled to my knees, nearly falling off the bed. I grabbed my reader and held it up towards the corner of the room. There it was, the network connection that kept flickering in and out.

A wave of dizziness knocked me back on the bed. I knelt there, every muscle shaking. My reader throbbed in my hands.

Where did you get this? It's connected to Wing 74's private wifi. It can access all of the base-level data.

I started to cry, whether from fear or joy I couldn't tell.

I'm not surprised you didn't notice. I doubt the range on the wifi is very far.

I threw up. Not figuratively, but literally, the cheap rug absorbing the splatter as I wretched a dozen emotions over the edge of the bed.

It can't be, I wanted to scream, but the more I considered it, the more I knew it really, truly could.

All the metal. The fake windows in Thames's office. The door panels. The data and devices magically resurrected from Wing 74.

There was a Gate B and a Gate C. It only stood to reason they'd be past Gate A.

Wiping my mouth on my sleeve, I grabbed my reader. Jayde had sent me more messages, but I didn't read them.

CAN YOU ADD EPHESUS TO GATE B OR GATE C?

YES. THEY HAVEN'T BEEN BLACKLISTED YET

I breathed roughly through my nose, praying wordlessly as I did so.

I'D RECOMMEND GATE C. BASED ON THE LOGS, THERE'S A LOT OF ACTIVITY ON THE OTHER SIDE OF GATE B. YOU'D PROBABLY

RUN INTO SOMEONE. WING C ISN'T VERY
BUSY

IT'S PROBABLY NOT FINISHED

I took his lack of comment as consent.

YOU SURE ABOUT THIS?

I nodded, even though he couldn't see me. I needed the
motion to anchor my courage.

I HAVE TO SEE FOR MYSELF

15

I paused in my doorway and glanced both ways. Nic had disappeared back into his room, and no one else was in sight. The entire wing was silent.

I glanced towards Gate C. Was now a good time? Should I wait until after dinner when everyone was off work and the power went into energy-saving mode? Or would that just raise more suspicion?

I realized, after regurgitating the thoughts through the logical part of my brain, that it didn't really matter when I did it. If I was honest with myself, I wasn't expecting my jailbreak to go undetected. My prints—or rather, my brother's—would be on the door's activity log, and I'm sure cameras were watching me right now. Thames would find out, sooner or later, that I'd accessed that door.

The trick was to stay one step ahead of him—and that meant I needed to act fast.

I swallowed one more prayer. Then I strode up to Gate C and flashed my hand across the sensor before I could think twice about it.

It shone green and opened.

I was so blinded by the sudden onslaught of natural light that I almost let the gate close again on my foot. The hallway beyond was gorgeous. To the right, the metal wall had been polished to a mirror-like shine. Sleek benches and trendy art speckled the length of it, and the floor was boldly decorated with irregular black and white tile. To the left, an archway of solid glass stretched from floor to ceiling, revealing a stunning view of the Martian countryside.

Somehow, my feet carried me up to the glass. It was nearing midday, and a halo of robin's egg blue surrounded the keyhole of light that was the distant sun. The rest of the sky was blurry like melted butterscotch, melding seamlessly with the dusty landscape. The view went for miles until it ended in an uncut plateau. The only movement was the flickering light on top of the nearest guidepost.

I knew what I would see. I knew, as soon as Jayde pulled up the door records, that we were on Mars. I knew this was Wing 74. But seeing it, splayed before me in undeniable color, was no less overwhelming.

My stomach flipflopped, as if suddenly realizing it had left Earth's gravity and needed to catch up. I sank to the floor on my knees and waited until the world came back into focus. A few tears—gentle ones—slipped down my cheek and dampened my lap.

"What now, God?" I said aloud.

A voice answered me, but it definitely wasn't God's.

"You really are a clever girl."

I whipped around, nearly falling over, and for a moment I could have sworn I was seeing a ghost. Not only had I never expected to see him again, but he was so slight and pale, with his aged hair and bleached lab coat, that it wouldn't have taken many special effects to turn him into a wraith.

"Carnegie," I said after I put a name with the face.

He nodded and drew his hand from his pocket. The reprogram disc for the door was clutched in his wrinkled fingers.

He snapped it on the panel next to Gate C and started fiddling with it.

I stood up, self-consciously straightening my skirt. "I thought you were dead."

He didn't answer. He didn't need to. "I could have sworn I fixed that glitch. But, as usual, you continue to provide invaluable product testing." He glanced at me, but he didn't seem particularly bothered.

I decided not to tell him I had help opening the door. "What are you doing here?"

"I never left."

"You work for Thames?"

He shot me an incredulous look over his shoulder. "Thames works for me."

It took only seconds for me to catch up. "It was you. It's always been you. You've been using Dr. Nic this whole time."

"He was a necessary evil. The original idea for Red Rain was his, although his execution had all the practicality of a science fiction novel." His lips twitched in a gesture too cruel to be called a smile. "His charisma was good in meetings, though. He was much better at getting sponsors than me."

He punched a button on the disc. The door beeped and whooshed shut. "There, that should be fixed now."

I sank onto a bench against the wall. Clearly, I wasn't going anywhere anytime soon. "How long have you been in charge?" I asked.

He pocketed the disc and sat down next to me, leaving a comfortable gap between us. "Long before your brother got involved. Who do you think pulled the strings to get Ephesus reassigned in the first place? Transferring unassimilated personnel is a *nightmare*. Nic never could have done it without me, not without raising huge red flags."

"So why'd you let him? Couldn't you have found another scientist?"

Carnegie shrugged. "Perhaps, but Nic had his whims, and it was to my advantage to let him think he was in charge." He gave me a conspiratorial smile, as if I were in on a secret. "That said, he was right on the money with your father. I always knew your brother couldn't do it—he was too young, too inexperienced. But your father had the best credentials of anyone I'd ever seen."

Every hair on my arms prickled. "How many scientists did you try?"

He groaned wearily. "Dozens."

"And did they all make it out alive?"

He frowned. "Child. What do you take me for? Most of them didn't get far enough to be given full access to the project. The few that did were paid off easily enough. I didn't have any trouble until your brother pulled his stunt." He chuckled, almost as if it were a fond memory. "Again, Nic is very lucky he had me to make that problem go away."

"So when I sent that email…"

He regarded me for a moment. "I underestimated you," he said without flattery or admiration. "I expected you to be too scared to do anything, or at least anything significant. I certainly didn't expect you to blow up a lab, escape, and alert the officials all within fifteen minutes."

I couldn't help but smile.

He didn't return the gesture. "Thankfully, the only person you contacted was Commander Ambrose, who was already on my payroll."

So Ambrose didn't find out about Red Rain when I alerted him; he already knew. A speck of guilt lifted from my soul and was immediately replaced by dread. Ambrose—and, by inference, Thames—had been involved all along. From the moment Ephesus was summoned to Mars, our lives had been pawns in his race to acquire Red Rain.

My whole body tightened, my hands coiling into fists at my side. Carnegie didn't notice. "After I generously granted him a 'raise,' he was very happy to forge some reports for me."

I thought about our blank files, and everything settled into place. That's why there was no record of our time on Mars. That's why they built the factory on Rott, an island in the middle of the ocean, even though it was gloriously impractical. That's why my multiple arrests and imprisonments had seemed strangely informal and involved shockingly little paperwork.

"So the United never did find out what happened up here," I said, for the first time in days feeling fully confident in my conclusion.

"They still haven't."

That's why Thames didn't want me to drop names on camera; they were trying to keep the Martian base clean. "So why involve Dr. Nic again? It seems like you finally had the opportunity to cut him from the picture. You could have left him on Rott to, well, you know."

Carnegie leaned his head against the wall. "I wanted to, believe me. But I still needed Red Rain. None of the other experimental weapons we've produced can even hold a candle to the tactical power of Red Rain."

He closed his eyes. "We tried for months to find another scientist to complete the work. No one even came close. Thames insisted we let Nic have another go at it. I knew he would be useless, but sometimes we compromise for our allies."

Realization filled my veins with ice. "Is that why you dragged my father back into it?"

He rolled his head and looked at me. "He was, quite frankly, our only hope. Nic tested him when he was up here, and the results were astonishing. I knew he could do it, given time and appropriate incentive."

Every nerve in my body flared. "So you kidnapped me and Cea to use as blackmail," I hissed, cramming as much bitterness and accusation as I could into every syllable.

He held my gaze. "You won't believe me when I say this, but I'm sorry it had to be this way."

"You're right, I don't believe you."

"I would have taken anyone else over your father. I knew he was emotionally unstable. After what he did to your mother, I knew he could be unpredictable and dangerous. But I thought that, if I had you, perhaps he could at least be controlled."

It was Carnegie who recommended it. He thought it would make your father more compliant if you two were together.

I shivered. Now I knew who had been watching me the whole time.

He laughed joylessly. "You see where that got me. First you blow up a lab and scare off my best scientists. Next, you destroy my multimillion-dollar factory and force me to drag you back up here to film a bunch of idiotic TikTok videos."

"What's TikTok?"

He shook his head. "Never mind, you're too young to remember." He rose. "We'd better be getting back now, or you'll miss lunch."

I warily stood up. "What are you going to do with me?"

He smiled benevolently. "My dear girl, you worry too much. Despite your flaws, you've proven to be very useful to me, and as long as you continue to play the part of my rising internet star, I won't let a hair on your head get hurt."

He gestured, and I reluctantly followed him back through Gate C. "Are you really going to let us go when you're done?" I prodded.

"Absolutely," he said without a moment's hesitation. "Once I've gotten everything I need, you'll be free to walk out those doors." He walked me back to my dorm. I opened the door and stepped inside.

"But once it's all said and done, I don't think you're going to want to leave."

I turned to look at him. He laid his hand on the frame to keep the door from closing.

"No, Philadelphia, I think once this is over, you're going to realize that you're safer with me."

He smiled, a cold, vicious smile that left no room for doubt: He was in control. And despite the fact that he had so graciously answered my questions, he had, in reality, told me nothing.

He let go of the doorframe. "You should try your coloring book. Thames picked it out especially for you."

He smiled at me until the door closed.

16

I stood there, staring at the door, long enough that it opened again to reveal Nic.

"Well?" he demanded without ceremony.

Thankfully I had spent the better part of the last fifteen minutes debating how to break the news to him and had reached the revolutionary conclusion that I should just state the facts.

"You know that ECV network with all the lab activity?"

"Yeah?"

"It's one of the private networks for Wing 74." I let that revelation bake for only a half-second before I added the icing on the cake. "And Carnegie says hi."

Nic was silent. I could tell by the way his eyes flickered that he was running the numbers and reaching the appropriate conclusions—at about triple the speed it had taken me.

After his eyebrows had run their full gamut of expressions, he turned, opened the door, and walked out.

"Where are you—"

He stopped in the middle of the hall and faced the corner. Then he flashed an obscene gesture and started vomiting a stream of words that were colorful even for him.

My door drifted shut, dampening his tirade only slightly. I waited. A few minutes later, he calmed down and came back in.

"I guess I know where the security camera in the hall is now," I offered.

Nic shrugged and smoothed his hair back into place.

I let curiosity steal the moment. "Did you have any idea it was him?"

He shot me a look. "If I had, we wouldn't be in this mess." He sighed and seemed to shuffle his emotions together like a stack of cards. "Well, the good news is that I'm now completely confident Carnegie doesn't have Red Rain. If he did, I'm pretty sure he would just bomb the United instead of posting those dumb videos. As it stands, it sounds like all he has is the Wing 74 data—which is out of date."

"Because it's such a secure network," I filled in the blanks.

"For better or for worse."

"So what now?" I put the obvious question on the table.

"No idea," he responded without hesitation. "Unfortunately we can't just walk out the front door—even if we could get the front door open."

I bit my lip. I hadn't considered that.

"I hate myself for saying this, but our best bet may be for you to finish recording the videos and see if he holds true to his promise."

I searched his face. "Do you think he'll keep his word?"

He returned my stare. "At this point, I don't want to bet on anything. But I would rather buy ourselves more time than try to blast out of here, guns blazing, without a plan. I'll take patience over death."

I had to agree on that point.

A thought came to me, and I rolled it around in my brain for a minute before sharing. "Should I try to drop hints in my videos about Carnegie and Mars? Maybe someone will pick up on it and—"

"Absolutely not," he interrupted in that all-too-familiar stern tone of voice. Only this time there was no bitterness in it—just genuine fear.

"Look, I may not have known Carnegie as well as I thought, but I do know one thing about him—he will kill. I've seen him do it. He's made it clear that we are both expendable, so if you outlive your usefulness, he will kill you without a second's thought."

I had no words. There was nothing to say; I knew he was right.

"I know you don't make a habit of listening to me..."

I frowned.

"...but this time, when I say 'keep your head down,' I really mean it."

I searched his face and found only honesty there. "Okay," I said after a moment.

He didn't look relieved by my consent. He probably didn't believe me.

I wasn't sure I believed me, either.

*

Carnegie joined us in the recording studio the next day.

I couldn't tell by Thames's reaction whether or not he had heard about my little breakout. He was startled that Carnegie showed up, but I think he was more uncomfortable with his boss hovering at his elbow than anything else.

Having Carnegie in my line of sight didn't make my job any easier, either. Every time I glanced up I found him staring at me, eyes unwavering. It was a constant reminder that he was in control and that each word I breathed was for his benefit. He was using me, and every second I was on air, I was making him stronger and more powerful.

It was also a warning about what would happen if I said anything out of line.

"Good job," he commended after I'd finished recording. It sounded like a genuine compliment, which was disgusting. "Let's do another session this afternoon. We don't want to keep your fans waiting after you've given them that delicious cliffhanger."

Two videos in one day? I involuntarily glanced at Thames, who was also visibly caught off-guard. *But why?*

I asked the same question of Nic at lunch.

"It's probably a power move," he replied without looking up. "Reminding you who's boss—since you have a habit of forgetting that."

I made a face at him, not that he caught it. "Or he's getting desperate. Which could be good for us."

"Or, more likely, it could be really bad for us."

I tried not to let that comment get to me as I walked back to the recording studio.

"Desperate" definitely seemed like an accurate description of Carnegie's behavior, not that his calm demeanor belayed any urgency. During our afternoon session, he made me record no less than five videos. Every time the stream would get cut off— which happened more quickly with each successive video—he would switch to another account and tell me to start over.

I narrated the end of my time on Mars and rolled right into the events of recent weeks—getting arrested, realizing I was being used as blackmail, breaking out with Cea. Every time I thought I'd reached a good stopping point, he would level his gaze on me, and I would have to suck in my breath and find the strength to keep going.

I think he would have made me recount the whole story in one sitting if Thames hadn't gathered the courage to interrupt him.

"Take a break, Philadelphia, and drink some water. I've stopped the stream," he said to me over the intercom. I gladly obeyed. As I chugged down the water, I watched them engage in a silent battle of the wills, staring each other down with increasing amounts of male dominance.

It was clear who had been pulling the strings the entire time. It must have been Carnegie's decision to send me to Rott—with or without Thames's consent.

To my surprise, Carnegie deferred. "Yes, I suppose that is enough for today." He turned his smile to me. "Rest up, Philli." He said the nickname with extra butter. "We'll do some more in the morning."

I avoided his gaze as the guards escorted me out.

When I returned to my room after dinner, Daddy was there to greet me.

Not in the flesh, of course—although if someone had taken my pulse at that moment, they might have thought it was really him. Instead, his face gazed out at me from a digital picture frame that had been propped on my nightstand next to a small planter of red flowers.

I cautiously stepped in and gazed around the room, wondering what else had been tampered with. The sheets looked like they had been changed and the rug vacuumed. My belongings were all there, but they had clearly been "tidied"—the position tweaked just enough to let me know that someone else had touched them.

I shivered, hoping that would shake the feeling of being violated from my nerves. Thankfully my reader had been on my person all day.

I walked up to the nightstand. I avoided my dad's eyes, instead studying the flowers. I recognized them instantly—it was the plant Mr. Sardis had given me when we arrived on Mars. He'd said I needed "a little color for my room," and it had sadly gotten left behind when we returned to Earth.

But he—or someone—had taken good care of it in my absence; it was blooming prolifically. Was Mr. Sardis still here? Did he know what was going on? Did he care?

I reached out and fingered the velvety leaves. To think I could be less than a hundred feet from friends and safety, and yet a few locked doors were keeping me from reaching them. It was infuriating and made me feel even more powerless and pathetic. Was this how Ephesus felt when he was imprisoned on Mars?

I swallowed and summoned the courage to look at the picture frame. It wasn't the most flattering picture of Daddy; it was professional, if not a bit stoic, probably scalped from an employee file. But it was still him, and the sight of him ignited a dozen emotions I didn't have the energy to deal with.

I wanted to feel sad, and lonely, and homesick. Those were safe emotions. I knew what they felt like, and I knew what to do with them. Those were the emotions I was *supposed* to be feeling.

The problem was that those weren't the only emotions I was feeling.

I picked up the frame and almost dropped it when the touch of my hand made the picture change unexpectedly. A profile of Ephesus appeared—another professional photo that had clearly been downloaded from somewhere.

I sat down on the bed and cycled through the images. Most of them were dated photos from the internet, but there were a few I'd never seen before. There were several shots of Ephesus that looked fairly new; had they been taken while he was on base? There was one of Dad that was definitely recent—I could tell by the creases under his eyes as he bent over his work in a lab I didn't recognize. Where had Carnegie gotten these?

I scrolled faster. And suddenly, there was Mama.

It was an old photo, taken before Ephesus was born. I could tell by the quality that it wasn't an original; it was probably something Dad had posted on his social media before the government had blocked his accounts.

Daddy and Mama posed in the picture together. They were somewhere bright and sunny, but the photo was zoomed in too closely to tell where. Their faces filled the frame nearly to the overflowing. Mama's sunlit hair spilled over her shoulders as she leaned her head on Daddy's chest. Her face sparkled with a laugh that was frozen in time.

Daddy's eyes were closed, and his face was buried in Mama's hair so deeply that you couldn't see his expression. But I could tell. I could tell by the crow's feet in the corners of his eyes and the flush in his cheeks: He was smiling.

A tear slid down my cheek. When was the last time Daddy had smiled like that? I shifted through my recent memory, scrolling through my own mental camera roll, trying to recall a moment in time when I had seen true joy on his face. I couldn't come up with one—not since Mama died.

I flinched, as I always did when I thought about Mama's death. But this time, my mind snagged on a different memory.

I would have taken anyone else over your father. I knew he was emotionally unstable. After what he did to your mother, I knew he could be unpredictable and dangerous.

The more I repeated Carnegie's words in my head, the more uncomfortable they made me—but not in the same way his other slimy behavior did. "After what he did to your mother"? Daddy hadn't *done* anything; the United was responsible for my mother's death. The situation was rather cut-and-dry: They accused her of a crime, and then they executed her. My dad had nothing to do with it.

Or did he?

The questions seeped into my mind. I tried to shove them away, but like a persistent leak, they continued to pile up. Did my father have something to do with Mama's death? Did something happen that day that he hadn't told me? What did Carnegie know that I didn't?

My reader buzzed in my pouch, and I realized that, for the first time in my life, I had the power to answer my own questions.

Setting the picture frame back on the nightstand, I pulled out my reader. Ignoring whatever notification had caused the alert, I pulled up the personnel file database and hacked in, just like Nic had taught me. Then with a deep breath, I hit search and typed *Abigail Smyrna*. Her picture was the third result.

In the nanosecond of lag between clicking on her image and the page loading, I flirted with irrational hope. I had never actually seen my mother's body. There had been no funeral. I only knew what I had been told, so maybe…

The air left me when the page loaded and I saw the bold word "DECEASED" branded at the top of her profile.

I stuffed my grief back down my throat and scrolled to the bottom. It was tempting to read her whole file, but I didn't have the emotional composure to handle the memories right now.

The last entry in her file was a yellow-bordered message, formatted differently than anything I'd seen before. I squinted at the header of the message.

Incident Flagged for Potential Police Misconduct. Investigation Status: Acquitted

I read the words again, slowly, letting them sink in. Police misconduct? Could it be that Mama's death had been ruled an accident?

The thought filled me with such dread that I couldn't breathe for a second. I suppose it should have made me feel better to know that it was all a mistake, that the United actually *wasn't* in the habit of executing people for coping Bibles. But instead it made me feel worse. The United had murdered my mother; the least they could do was own up to it and not have the *audacity* to call it an accident.

Anger turned my knuckles white, but I kept reading.

On October 11th, 2072, an investigation into a possible account of police misconduct was opened regarding an incident that occurred on October 10th at the Street 87 Reassimilation Services Compound. Police had been dispatched with a warrant to arrest Dr. Thomas Smyrna [husband of the deceased] for the charges of transmitting illegal media.

Time stopped—or, more accurately, it stumbled. Reality seemed to dip off-kilter as I processed that sentence.

My father had said that Mama was the one charged with transmitting. But it wasn't her; it was him. He was the one they had come to arrest.

You lied, Daddy.

The universe restarted, and faster. I gripped the reader and held it a hairbreadth from my nose as I fought to read the rest of the file as quickly as possible. My eyes kept tripping over each other, and I had to reread the words over and over before my brain understood them.

Mrs. and Dr. Smyrna were home when officers arrived. Dr. Smyrna resisted arrest. Officers drew weapons in an attempt to subdue him, and Abigail Smyrna was unintentionally shot. She died of her injuries en route to the hospital.

I felt sick. All I could see was Mama, my precious, innocent Mama, bleeding out, her blood filling the grout in our entryway like a river—my beloved Mama, draped over a stretcher, sirens wailing as her life slipped away.

And Dad, kneeling on the floor, viciously attempting to scrub the blood from the tile before I got home. *Oh, Daddy...*

Officials reviewed all available evidence, including bodycam footage and Dr. Smyrna's own confession, and determined that the officers had acted appropriately. The fatal shooting was clearly caused by direct interference from Dr. Smyrna as he attempted to grab an officer's weapon.

I tried to picture the scene, but I couldn't. I couldn't imagine my placid father punching an officer in the face and going for his gun. I couldn't imagine my father using a weapon at all. My father wouldn't resist arrest. That was not the Dr. Smyrna I knew.

Or thought I knew.

All charges against the officer were dropped. In light of Dr. Smyrna's compliance with the investigation, officials rescinded the arrest warrant and issued a warning. All affected personnel files have been appropriately updated.

My reader hit the floor. I didn't bother to pick it up and instead wrapped my arms around my chest—tighter, tighter—as if by squeezing myself I could keep my world from shattering. It didn't make any sense. That's not how it happened—that's not what Daddy had told me.

And yet as my mind involuntarily replayed that day—and the weeks, months, years that followed—it tripped over all the clues I should have seen. All the signals I had missed in my delirious grief: the premeditated speeches, the resignation, the calculated tones of voice. The guilt.

Well, Dr. Smyrna, coming around, are we? You used to be the troublesome one.

And then, like a torn sweater unraveling, I watched my father regress. I saw the lines deepen under his eyes, the frown hardening on his lips. I remembered how his attitude and actions had changed—bit by bit, day by day. Here a little compromise, there a little surrender. The slow retreat.

I'm surprised your father didn't offer any objections, Phil.

We talked about it, last night. He said it wasn't worth the blood right now.

Oh the talks—we had so many talks. Always explaining, always justifying, always moving a little more out of the way to try and keep me—or himself—from getting hurt.

Philadelphia, it's the only way! There's nothing I can do... nothing!

Suddenly I was back in that alley. Stanyard's car was smashed against a dumpster, and Ephesus was bleeding in the front seat. There were sirens, and screaming—probably mine— and Stanyard yelling at me to run. And through it all cut my father's cold voice, telling me to stay put until the officers arrived.

I'm not letting either of you get hurt anymore.

He'd turned himself in. I understood that now. He'd chosen not to run—perhaps because he was afraid that if I ran down that alley, I might get shot in the back, just like Mama had.

And maybe, just maybe, that was why he had agreed to create Red Rain.

Just go.

I cried. Curled up on the bed in the tiniest ball I could manage and sobbed. The tears poured out of me, rolling off my nose and clogging my throat. Faster and faster they kept coming as I shed years of lies, manipulation, and guilt onto the blanket.

Why, Daddy, why?

Why did you do it?

Why did you lie to me?

Eventually my tears slowed enough that I could hear around the throbbing in my ears. The air in the room shifted, as if the Holy Spirit had sat down on the bed next to me. My final tears slid out silently as I strained to wrap my nerves around that feeling, as if by holding my breath I could pull Him closer.

Why, Daddy? The question wafted through my consciousness again. *Why did you do it?*

He should have—what should he have done? Should he have gone quietly? Fought harder? Been more careful? I didn't know— I couldn't even process the million alternate scenarios that were spiraling just out of reach in the realm of what-if.

But he should have told me. He should have told me the truth. He should have told me why. Why wasn't he resisting Commander Ambrose? Why did he agree to go to Mars? Why did he make Red Rain? Maybe, if he had told me the truth, we could have been fighting together—instead of against each other.

I sat up slowly. My center of balance was off, as if I'd shed part of my mass through my tears. I bent down and retrieved my reader off the floor.

I brushed the screen off and tabbed back to my Bible. It was open to Matthew.

I clutched the device to my chest. There was only one way to end this.

17

Narissa had her work cut out for her in the morning. Between the constant crying (the tears never really stopped all night) and staying up late praying, my face was a train wreck.

But for once, I didn't *feel* like a train wreck. I was scared—terrified, even. I had no idea how I was going to get the words out around the bleeding emotions that hadn't scabbed over. I didn't know if Carnegie would let me say what I needed to say. Was my dad even listening to the streams? But despite the fact that I was weak and exhausted, my heart felt strangely calm as I walked into the recording studio and arranged myself in front of the camera.

Carnegie was in the control booth again. "Pick up where you left off yesterday and just keep going," he instructed. "I'll tell you when to stop."

There was no room for argument in that statement. I just nodded and took a moment to regulate my breathing. *In, out. In, out.*

Thames glanced at both of us uneasily before starting the countdown. I closed my eyes and did my own countdown—*in, out, in, out*—praying in time with the beat.

When Thames gave the go-ahead, I opened my eyes and looked directly into the camera.

"Hey Dad. I know what happened with Mama."

I glanced at the control booth. This was it—this was their opportunity to cut me off. Thames lurched forward, finger reaching towards the button, but Carnegie laid a hand on his arm to stop him. His eyes were watching me, as they always were.

I turned away from him and focused my attention squarely on the camera lens. I tried to imagine my father's face reflected on the curved glass, channeling all my energy into getting the words out.

"I looked up her file and read the official report. I'm sure it didn't happen exactly like they said, but—I think it's close enough to the truth. And..."

I sucked in a breath. *Holy Spirit, I need you* now.

"I think I understand."

Another breath. *Don't leave me.*

"I think I know why... Why we stopped arguing with the commander. Why I started going to school without complaint. Why you didn't fight back when they sent Ephesus away, and then you. Why you told me to 'be discrete' and 'obey' and 'not cause trouble.' Why you didn't want us to run from the officials. Why you let them send me to prison. Why you worked on..."

I'll never know if Carnegie would have stopped me from saying "Red Rain," because my pain did it for him. The emotion exploded out of me in an ugly sob. I hid my face as tears swam in my eyes, making my eyeliner sting.

I took a deep breath, but there was no damming the emotions now. "I'm scared, Dad," I cried, my voice garbled with another sob. I forced myself to look back into the camera, even though I was squinting through the tears. "I feel—I feel like I don't know you anymore. You abandoned me, you really did. You left me with those men and just *walked away!*"

My voice cracked in a scream. I looked to the ceiling and gulped several lungfuls of air. "'Just go,' you said. Not 'goodbye' or 'I'll come find you' or even 'I'm sorry.' 'Just go.' How could you?" The question came out in a squeaky whisper, but I didn't repeat it. I didn't have the strength to.

"I'm scared," I said again. "I'm frightened and I feel alone and I'm questioning everything you did and I don't know if I can trust you. I don't. I really don't."

I swallowed. It was done. I had done what he—what both of us—had been unwilling to do for so long: I told the truth.

I felt the Holy Spirit stirring deep inside of me like a river. "But." I pressed the heels of my hands to my eyes; they came away smeared with mascara. I stared at them for a minute, gathering all my courage to say the hardest three words of my life.

"I forgive you."

Seventy times seven.

I looked into the camera and said it again, louder this time.

"I forgive you, Dad. I forgive you for lying, and I forgive you for what happened with Mama. Maybe it was a mistake—maybe you shouldn't have resisted. Or maybe it really was just an accident."

I winced as the word left my lips. It still stung—bitterly—to call Mama's death an accident, like I was forfeiting the one grievance I had been able to hold onto for so many years. But it felt right. It was right.

"I'll never know if you did the right thing or not. I wasn't there, and that's... that's okay. I don't have to know if it was right or not." My voice grew clearer as the revelation flowed through me. "I don't have to decide that. I don't have to judge."

The Spirit was pressing so hard against my chest that it hurt. I sat up straight.

"But I do know we're not there now. This is not that moment. Maybe it was a mistake, maybe it wasn't, but we can't keep looking back and basing all our decisions on what happened then."

I leaned forward, my eyes searching the camera. "You can't keep giving in—*we* can't keep giving in. Look where it's got us. We should have run down that alley—ran and kept running. We have to fight, Dad. Fight for our family, fight for freedom, fight for people who can't fight for themselves. We can't let them win."

I glanced at Thames and Carnegie out of the corner of my eye. Both men were still watching me in silence.

"They *can't* win. We can't surrender, not this time. I'm not going to let them keep using me."

Carnegie didn't even blink.

"Help me, Dad. Fight with me. Don't let them use you. Don't let them blackmail you. Whatever they tell you, whatever they say they're going to do to me, don't listen. Don't let them win. Don't let them have—"

The forbidden name died on my tongue as all the air evaporated from the room.

No, Philadelphia, I think once this is over, you're going to realize that you're safer with me.

I met Carnegie's gaze. He stared back, eyes like ice.

I hate to break it to you, but if they get your father in the same room with this data, he could reconstruct the formula.

I turned to the camera, where the playback screen reflected my horror in high definition.

Despite your flaws, you've proven to be very useful to me.

On the bright side, we'll know the minute your family is found. The entire government is searching for them.

They saw my video.

Pain ripped through me. "I've been leading you right to him."

It was barely a whisper, but Thames heard. I saw him scrambling in the control booth and knew I only had seconds.

"Don't do it, Dad!" I screamed, lunging towards the camera. "Don't come for me! They're using me to get—"

The last sound the world heard was my strangled scream as Carnegie's fingers closed around my throat.

18

I hit the floor, gasping. Carnegie had kept his fingers around my throat until he was sure I wasn't going to resist, then dragged me down the hall by my collar. By the time we reached whatever room he threw me into, I had convinced myself that I was going to die. I knelt there, hacking, trying to force air back into my lungs, but breathing felt like dragging a heavy dresser across the floor. It was like my throat had been crushed and no air could get through.

He was talking, but I couldn't hear him around the throbbing and flashing colors. I pressed my forehead to the floor, forcing my breaths to become smaller and slower. I waited until the burn subsided and the panic faded from the edges of my vision before I looked up at him.

"You monster," I rasped.

Whatever he had been saying apparently wasn't important enough to repeat, because he just crossed his arms and glared at me.

I carefully swallowed, trying to get some volume back into my voice. "You want Red Rain." I had to hear it from him; I had to know I was right. "That's why you're using me. That's why you needed those videos to go viral. You're trying to find my dad."

"Such a clever girl, as always. I figured if he didn't try to make contact with you, he would get picked up by the United somewhere—and I have contacts who will be happy to sell him back to me."

"It won't work." My voice still sounded like sandpaper, but it was full of confidence.

"Won't it?" He walked to the door and started fiddling with the panel. "I'm sure *you* won't be cooperative, but I have high hopes for your father. I still have his favorite incentive—and after that stunt you just pulled, I'm sure he knows exactly how much danger you're in."

I winced. He was right, but Dad—if he was watching—also heard the rest of my stream. He knew what I wanted, what I *needed* from him, and maybe, just maybe, he was listening.

Not this time, God. Give him courage!

"I'm not going to let you do this," I challenged, and I meant it.

The panel hissed at him. He glanced over his shoulder at me. "And just what are you going to do about it?"

I didn't hesitate. "I'll figure something out."

He sighed. "That's what I was afraid of." He tapped a button on the panel, and it screeched and went dark. Then he reached into his pocket and turned to face me.

A loaded syringe lay in his hand.

My heart leapt to my throat, but I swallowed it. I clenched my jaw and my fists.

"On second thought..." Carnegie rolled the syringe around in his palm for a second, then dropped it back in his pocket. "I want you to tell your sweet boyfriend that you have three days to live."

My thoughts crashed to a stop, unable to process that statement on the first try. Thankfully, he repeated himself.

"Tell him that unless your father or your brother makes contact with me in the next 72 hours, I will kill you."

The panic rolled back in. Did he really think we'd been in contact with my father? "But how—"

"Don't play dumb with me!" he shouted, for the first time his voice changing octaves. "Don't you think I know you've been chatting with that boyfriend of yours online?"

I flushed all sorts of colors as horror filled my nerves. "You've been monitoring my reader?"

"I've been monitoring everything," he snapped. He sighed and resumed his usual monotone. "And yes, I know all about the 'help' you had with the doors. Believe me, when I find out who your boyfriend is, I'll invite you to the hanging."

I swallowed rapidly to suppress the fear. I didn't have time to be scared right now—I needed to focus. Something wasn't adding up. "If you knew I was online, why didn't you pull the plug? You could have taken my reader away, or changed the access codes, or something."

He frowned at me over his nose. "Because I was hoping you'd do exactly what you did—try and make contact with your father. Why do you think I made it so easy for Nic to get onto the internet? Let me spell it out for you: If Nic can hack into it, the door wasn't locked in the first place."

I shivered.

"The doors, though… I have to give it to you on that one." He ran a hand through his bleach-white hair. "I really thought I'd fixed that glitch, but you played me for a fool yet again."

"Then why didn't you take Gate C offline or something?"

He scoffed. "It wasn't worth the effort. It was much easier just to blacklist your father and brother."

Several of my escape plans evaporated at that statement.

"But, just in case, I've disabled this panel."

I looked up at him. He gestured over his shoulder at the darkened panel. "This door will only open from the outside now. So feel free to have your friends tinker with the lock all you want—it won't help you. In fact…"

He took a step towards me. I instinctively slid back.

"Let's send a message to your friends, shall we? Pull out your reader."

I didn't.

"Don't you want to let them know you're okay? I'm sure they're worried sick about you."

It wasn't a suggestion. I slowly slid my reader from my pouch.

"I want you to send a message to both of them and tell them they have three days to find your father. You have five minutes before I cut your internet off. Use them wisely."

He stepped out into the hall and tapped the exterior panel. The door hissed shut and locked with a beep.

I waited until his footsteps retreated before opening the messaging app. I was instantly assaulted with a dozen notifications. Jayde had been texting me nonstop. Nic had texted me once.

YOU GOOD?

I typed back.

FOR NOW. CARNEGIE SAYS WE HAVE 3 DAYS TO FIND MY FATHER BEFORE HE KILLS ME

There was a beat. I steeled myself for a sarcastic "I told you so" response, but instead he sent two words I never expected to hear from him.

I'M SORRY

I pondered the screen for a moment before remembering I was running out of time. I sent a hasty "thank you" message back and hoped he could infer the rest.

I switched over to Jayde and skimmed the message history. It was clear he had been watching the stream and couldn't decide whether to be mad or worried.

A new message popped up even as I was reading.

I CAN TELL YOU'RE ONLINE. ANSWER ME

I'M SORRY. I'M FINE

He sent back a message that, run through a profanity filter, would read *"What in the world were you thinking?"*

NO TIME TO EXPLAIN. CARNEGIE IS GOING TO CUT MY INTERNET IN A FEW MINUTES

WHO?

YOU NEED TO RUN—HE'S BEEN LISTENING TO OUR CONVERSATIONS. HE'S LOOKING FOR YOU

I CAN TAKE CARE OF MYSELF. IT'S YOU I'M WORRIED ABOUT. WHAT'S HE GOING TO DO WITH YOU?

No sense in sugar-coating it.

IF MY FATHER OR BROTHER DOESN'T MAKE CONTACT WITHIN 3 DAYS, HE'S GOING TO KILL ME

The typing dots appeared immediately—and then cycled indefinitely. I waited one beat, two, before I realized the message was never going to come. Carnegie had pulled the plug.

I glanced down at the taskbar and was surprised to find I still had three bars of service.

What's wrong? I clicked on the connections menu. NCC1701D and Wing B Guest were grayed out, but ECV197 was glowing strong.

Wing 74.

I stood up and looked around the room for the first time. It looked a lot like the room Nic had thrown me into six months ago when I'd broken out of Wing 74; it could even be the same one.

But wherever it was, it was deeper into the wing, which meant I could freely connect to the network.

Carnegie must not know my reader was connected to Wing 74. I replayed my conversations with Nic and Jayde and realized I'd never said my reader was connected to ECV197; I'd only mentioned it as one of the many networks in range. Carnegie had no idea I was on here.

Hope soared through my veins—and then crashed off the edge like a waterfall. Wing 74's wifi was a highly secure internal network; there was no way to access the internet through it. I knew that from experience.

I sat down on the bench bolted to the wall and toggled to the file menu. As I expected, a lengthy list of cryptically scientific folders appeared. I leaned back and studied it, for the first time fully aware of what I was holding. This was Carnegie's war: The remnants of Red Rain, plus a dozen other weapons designed to beat Earth into submission.

My fingers tensed as I fought the urge to start aggressively deleting files. Carnegie could surely recover them, and as soon as he saw that someone was tampering with the database, he would figure out my reader was connected and take me offline. Or he'd just kill me.

I sighed and leaned my head against the unforgiving metal wall. There had to be *something* I could do. I held his entire empire in my hands; surely there was some way to set it on fire.

We let it burn.

It came to me in a rush. The sirens, the coursing lights, the factory shrieking and wailing as it self-destructed, all its systems thrown into a panic.

The virus.

I instinctively looked at my shoe. Thames had taken my flash drive—which meant Carnegie had it. Surely he'd looked at it and copied over anything that was useful to him. And where else would he store his weapons but Wing 74?

I ran several searches and couldn't find it. My flash of brilliance faded as quickly as it had flared; maybe Carnegie was using a different server. Nic had said this database hadn't been updated—

Until recently. Jayde had said there was new activity.

I pulled up "recent files"—and there it was. Carnegie had renamed it, but I recognized the file extension.

I clicked on it, and my device screeched in warning. A prompt consumed the screen, asking if I wanted to allow the program to make changes to my device. I hesitated with my thumb on the "run" button.

I had seen what this virus did to the factory. Every system had gone into a tailspin as the virus consumed programs in a tidal wave of chaos. There was no telling what would happen when I released this virus onto a space station, which was an even more delicately balanced machine than a factory of lethal chemicals. For all I knew, the virus would take the habitat systems offline and suck all the oxygen out of the room.

Of course, if a system glitch didn't kill me, Carnegie would be happy to finish the job.

I pulled my hand away from the screen. This stunt wouldn't save me. There was no guarantee it would stop Carnegie, either. He'd still have the base, and he'd still have Thames and his money. He could rebuild. He could still try to find my father.

But without Wing 74's data, he'd be starting from scratch. No matter how much government funding he had, it would still take him a long time to reconstruct ten years of labor.

If he wants Red Rain, I'm going to make him work for it.

I closed my eyes and prayed. I prayed for my dad, for Ephesus, for Cea, for Nic—all the people I would never be able to tell goodbye.

And then, without even a flicker of hesitation, I opened my eyes and hit "run."

19

At first, nothing happened, and my adrenaline fizzled out like a dead firecracker when it realized it had nothing to stick to. Did I do it right? Did I miss a step? Was there an art to launching viruses?

I clicked on the program again, and my screen flashed with an all-too-familiar warning:

Error: File not found.

I smiled.

I backed out, and the whole folder vanished beneath my fingertips. I clicked on a few other directories and found the same thing.

My device started to lag. A few more clicks, and the whole screen glitched. I tapped it rapidly, but it was bricked. The virus had done its job.

I turned off the device and slid it back into my pouch, even though I realized, with some grief, that it was now a glorified paperweight.

Now what? Surely it wouldn't take Carnegie long to realize what was happening, and if he was as smart as he appeared, it would only take him a second more to conclude that I'd done it. He'd be coming for me; I had minutes, at best.

In spite of myself, my heartbeat started to escalate. At least I knew who would be waiting for me on the other side of death.

I got up and walked to the door, listening. There were no angry shouts, no footsteps—but I did hear a faint beeping.

I pressed my ear to the door. It sounded like it was coming from the other side of the access panel. I'd never heard a door make that sound before, but it was annoyed and incessant—like an error message.

I remembered the frozen dials and throbbing displays on the machines in the factory. If the virus could send a factory into overtime, maybe it could cause the door locks to malfunction.

A light of hope flickered on in my chest, and all my adrenaline clung to it.

I stepped back and regarded the door. Didn't they say you should always push on an automatic door in an emergency?

Steeling my nerves, I threw all my weight into the center of the door with my shoulder. It didn't open—I moaned as the force shuddered back through me—but it felt different. It felt loose, almost as if the hydraulics were no longer holding the panels in place.

I scraped at the seam with my fingernails, struggling to get a handhold. I felt the panels shift.

"Jesus, come on!" I screamed through gritted teeth. I hissed as my fingers slipped on the sharp metal edge. Ignoring the smears of blood across the door, I crammed my fingers into the seam and shoved. With a labored groan, the doors slid open a few inches.

I pried my shoulder in, then my knee. With a strangled cry, I pushed with everything I had. Metal scraped on metal as the doors shuddered open.

I stumbled into the hall. A quick glance showed me the hall was empty, but surely not for long.

I pressed my wounded palms against my jacket, trying to think past the pain and survival instincts. The irritated beeping of the door panels rippled down the hall, completely out of sync from one another. I could pry any one of these doors open right now, but my bloody handprints would give Carnegie a clear trail to follow. I needed to put as much distance as possible between us and then find place to hide—or find a way out of Wing 74 where maybe I could get help.

It was a fifty-fifty chance which way he'd come down the hall. I mentally cast lots and chose the left.

I ran as fast as I could without thundering. I strained to hear any sound over my footsteps and the erratic beeping. I heard a shout and nearly tripped over myself in panic, but it sounded like it was echoing from far away, so I kept going.

I rounded a corner and screeched to a stop just in time. At the far end of the hall, a door was open. The light—and agitated voices—from within spilled out into the corridor.

I spun around. I had to duck in somewhere, fast. Doubling back down the hall, I chose the biggest door; maybe if I went into a hall with more doors, I could lead them astray.

I held my breath and wedged my fingers in the door, hoping they couldn't hear my grunting. I slipped through and immediately realized I'd made a mistake.

The hall was silent; all of the access panels were lit and intact. This wing must be on a different system. It hadn't been affected by the virus, which meant I was trapped.

Was it too late to turn back? Or would it be safer to hide and wait until the coast was clear?

I scanned the hall, looking for an alcove, and a familiar red sign caught my eye:

On Air.

The recording studio. I'd been able to open the door the other day, either because it wasn't locked or because it was set to accept me. Hopefully one of those things was still true.

I ran to the door and flapped my hand over the panel. It opened agreeably.

I slipped in and waited for the door to shut behind me. The room was just as I'd left it half an hour ago. All the lights were on and the camera was still running. The viewscreen showed a crystal-clear image of the toppled chair and torn greenscreen.

I glanced towards the control booth and saw that it was mercifully empty. It, too, had been hastily abandoned; all the monitors were up and running. My last stream was paused on one screen, my terrified but determined stare ominously frozen.

My heart rate began to tick in time with a different beat. *There's one way to make sure Carnegie never rebuilds.*

I turned back to the door. I put my ear to the seam and listened. When I heard nothing, I opened it and ran to the control booth. It, too, opened without complaint.

I shoved the desk chair out of my way and approached the monitor. I took one glance and decided I didn't have time to decode the labyrinth of controls needed to run the camera. I would have to use something simpler. I searched the desk and found Thames's abandoned tablet.

I picked it up and flipped through the open apps. One was a video streaming service. I clicked on it. He'd run a search using the terms "blue fire."

What's "blue fire"? I refreshed the results, and hundreds of videos popped up—most of which had my name in the title.

Whatever "blue fire" was, it had something to do with my videos, and it was an insanely popular upload tag. Thames hadn't been lying when he said I was trending.

I clicked on Thames's profile. It was a dummy account; there was no profile picture, and all the details looked fake. There were no posted videos. But the "Go Live" button glowed welcomingly, bright and red.

I tapped it, and it prompted me to add a title and description. I put the juiciest title I could think of—"Philadelphia tells the truth about what happened on Rott"—then barfed a couple of hashtags into the description.

#REDRAIN #SMYRNA #BLUEFIRE

Satisfied, I hit "next." The tablet's camera flickered on. The screen showed me a preview of what my stream would look like, and I cringed at the sight of my own reflection. My face was a mess of mascara and blood.

I pulled down my sleeve and gave my face a quick swipe, then coughed to clear my throat. I had to talk fast to get out what I needed to say before someone found me—or the United cut off my stream.

Although, once they heard what I had to say, they would probably let me through.

I centered myself in the frame and hit "start." The player counted down—*3, 2, 1*—then glowed red. I spoke as loud as I dared into the empty room.

"My name is Philadelphia Smyrna, and I'm here to tell you what really happened on Rott."

My viewer count ticked in the corner of the screen. It started at 1 and slowly started to climb—5, 18, 33.

"That factory was making an extremely lethal weapon called Red Rain. It's like manufactured acid rain, but worse."

My count reached the low 100s, then stagnated. Had I used the right hashtags? *You've gotta do this, Jesus!*

I pressed on. "It's a gas that can turn any kind of water or precipitation into an acid strong enough to melt metal—and kill anything that breathes. They were going to use it against the United."

I hesitated. *Who's "they"?* I had to incriminate Carnegie, and concisely—which was a problem, because they probably had no idea who Carnegie was. Even Jayde hadn't known Carnegie by name. I could tell them about the Martian base, but Carnegie would be long gone before they could get here.

My viewer count tripled. I needed to tell the United exactly where to look, and fast.

And then I remembered—there was someone else involved. Someone who was already in hot water with the officials.

"Their contact is a government agent named Thames. He has an office somewhere in the Boston metropolitan area. He's the one who kidnapped me and blackmailed my father into completing the formula. He was the one monitoring Rott. If you trace the data virus, you'll find it leads straight back to him."

My viewers skyrocketed—at the same time the door hissed open.

I whipped around. Thames stood in the hall.

I gaped at him, startled but somehow unafraid. There was nowhere to run, even if my nerves had been willing to cooperate.

"What have you done?" he said, barely a whisper.

I didn't answer.

His eyes fell on the tablet in my hands, which was still streaming. "You've ruined me."

Abruptly I realized he was crying.

The big guys are looking for blood.

He stepped into the room. I stumbled back into the desk, causing a monitor to rock precariously.

"You have no idea what you've done!" he screeched.

But I did know. I knew exactly what I'd done.

I straightened. "You ruined yourself."

His eyes searched me angrily. "You don't understand. I could have *helped* you!"

"You could never help me."

He roared. He lurched forward and yanked a desk drawer open, withdrawing a gun.

I screamed. The tablet clattered to the floor.

Thames cocked the weapon. Tears were coursing down his face as he drank me in one last time. "We would have loved you!" he yelled, and leveled the gun.

I threw my hands over my head. Five seconds too late, I realized he wasn't pointing the gun at me.

20

Thames slumped over, slowly, as if he still had enough vitality left to guide his fall. His body collapsed into the desk chair, sending it crashing into the wall.

I waited until the chair had stopped spinning and my ears had stopped ringing and he had stopped breathing before I moved.

I gingerly stepped forward—right into a pool of blood.

Suddenly I could smell it, see it, almost *hear* it pouring out onto the metal floor. I tasted bile.

Against every fiber of my being, I bent over and pried the gun from his still-warm hand. I slid it in my pocket, where it thumped against my thigh like a brick. Choking on a sound between a gag and a sob, I snatched the tablet from the floor and darted out of the room.

There was no one in the corridor. I ran to the gate, marked by my bloody handprints, and glanced around the hall beyond.

No one came running. There was no sound at all except for the obnoxious beeping echoing from the broken door panels like a dying heart monitor.

Where was Carnegie? Had he made a run for it? Or had he also—

I didn't want to think about it. I needed help. I needed to find Nic.

All I had to do was retrace my steps from the recording studio—I'd walked that way enough times before. I closed my eyes, and immediately I saw everything I didn't want to see—Carnegie with a syringe in his hand, me with blood on my palms, Thames with a bullet in his...

Jesus Jesus Jesus, was all I could think to pray.

I forced myself to start walking. I found Gate B, which was still online.

I panicked. I had no way to contact Nic or Jayde; the messaging app was on my reader, which was useless. All I had was Thames's tablet.

Which no doubt had the door lock software on it. And Thames had level 1 security clearance.

It took longer than it should have. My hands were shaky and my fingers slippery with sweat. My mind was spinning and struggling to process even the simplest tasks without seeing flashing colors and imagining disembodied screams. But with no small amount of help from the Holy Spirit, I managed to find the door lock software and whitelist Nic and myself.

Nic must have heard my muttering and broken sobs, because he was waiting on the other side of the door when I finally got it opened.

"Show me," he demanded.

I led him back to the recording studio, even though every nerve in my body recoiled in horror. I swear I could smell it— him—all the way out in the hall.

Nic took one look inside the control booth and immediately assumed command. In a blink the old governor returned. He let us into a nearby office, where he commanded me to wait.

I gratefully did so. I curled up on the chair in front of the desk and numbly watched as he started making calls.

Ten minutes later, he left, telling me not to move. I had no intention of doing so. I pulled my knees to my chest and rocked back and forth. I wasn't crying—I wasn't sure if I wanted to cry—but I had to do something, execute some repetitive motion, or I was certain I was going to crack under the emotional pressure.

What were we going to do now? Where was Carnegie? Had the United seen my stream? Would they find Thames's office? What about Jayde? What would—

"Philli."

I screamed and fell out of the chair, where thick arms caught me. I panicked and fought—until I realized the hands holding me were large, black, and crusted with potting soil.

I looked up into his face. "Mr. Sardis?"

His pained eyes squinted at me, and he opened his arms for a hug. I threw myself into them. I grabbed him around the neck like an anchor and sobbed, releasing all the fear and terror in an unfiltered stream.

He let me cry until I paused to breathe again. Then he stood up and put his hand on my shoulder. "Let's get you home."

I vainly rubbed my eyes as we took the long trek back from Wing 74 to the front of the base. The sense of familiarity grew like heat rising in an oven as we neared the dorms. I couldn't tell if it made me feel more at home or further away from it.

He let me back into our old dorm. I sank down on the couch and looked around at the familiar furniture, trying to scrape together a feeling other than emptiness. I couldn't find anything.

Mr. Sardis returned a half-hour later with all my baggage, including my colored pencils. I shoved them to the bottom of my suitcase, intending to deal with them later and knowing I probably never would. I grabbed my toiletries and did the only thing I knew how to do—shower and pray. Even if the prayers didn't wash away the sense of horror, at least the water would wash away the blood.

Around six, my doorbell rang. I answered it to find a stunning black woman I only vaguely remembered—Mr. Sardis's wife.

"We want you to eat with us," she said with a gentle smile.

I didn't argue. I sat with them in the cafeteria, letting their young son entertain me with his constant jabbering. I didn't eat much, but I soaked in everything. The smell of food. The dying sunlight soaking through the windows. The bright plastic. The ambiance of people—other people. It felt like it had been so long since I'd been in community with other people. I listened to their talking, the clattering of their silverware, their laughter. I let it seep into my veins like an IV, bringing a small trickle of life back to my soul.

I wasn't quite ready to be alone for the night, but the Sardis's seemed to have thought of that. Their son dragged me back to their dorm, where we sat on their couch and watched episode after episode of his favorite TV show. We watched until he passed out on my lap and his dad carried him to bed.

Mrs. Sardis walked me back to my dorm. "Ring if you need anything—any time of night."

I thanked her with a hug.

A brand-new tablet lay on the couch. I picked it up. It was light and razor-thin, and the screen blinked to life at the sight of my face. Only three programs had been installed: the messaging app, an ereader, and a music player.

I clicked on the messaging app and saw two new texts from Nic.

I COPIED MY MEDIA ARCHIVE TO THIS DEVICE. I HOPE THAT WILL SUFFICE

I smiled, then saw the second message.

CARNEGIE IS TAKEN CARE OF. I'LL EXPLAIN IN THE MORNING

For once, I was all too grateful to accept his explanation and leave it alone. I curled up on the couch and opened a chat with Jayde.

HEY

His response was instant.

I'VE BEEN TRYING TO REACH YOU FOR HOURS

I glanced back at the message history and realized that was true.

SORRY

I started to explain, and then realized I didn't want to.

DID YOU SEE MY STREAM?

WHY DO YOU THINK I'M FREAKING OUT?

I winced.

IT'S FINE. I'M FINE. THAMES IS DEAD. NIC TOOK CARE OF CARNEGIE

I licked my lips and hoped he wouldn't ask for further explanation. He didn't. There was a long pause before he responded at all.

I THOUGHT I LOST YOU

I typed back another "I'm sorry," even though I didn't know exactly what I was apologizing for. I didn't regret any of my actions, and I would do it all again if it meant keeping Red Rain out of the hands of Thames and Carnegie.
I redirected the conversation back at him.

WHAT ARE YOU GOING TO DO? THE UNITED IS PROBABLY GOING TO BUST THAMES'S OFFICE, YOU NEED TO GET OUT OF THERE

The typing dots appeared, vanished, and reappeared again several times before a message came through.

DON'T WORRY ABOUT ME, I'M LONG GONE

WHAT ARE YOU GOING TO DO FOR WORK?

This time, there was a good minute of silence before he responded.

I'LL BE FINE. THE THING ABOUT THAMES IS THAT HE WASN'T ALL UP-AND-UP WITH THE UNITED. SINCE HE WAS IN THE HABIT OF FORGING PAPERWORK HIMSELF, IT'S A LOT EASIER FOR SOMEONE WITH FAKE CREDENTIALS—LIKE ME—TO SLIP IN HIS RANKS. I'LL HAVE MY FILE SCRUBBED BY MORNING, AND THEN I CAN JUST GET ANOTHER JOB

I smiled and thanked God.

I'M REALLY HAPPY TO HEAR THAT

GET SOME REST. WE CAN TALK TOMORROW

OKAY. THANK YOU AGAIN FOR ALL YOUR HELP. I COULDN'T HAVE DONE IT WITHOUT YOU

He didn't respond for an unusually long time. I began to wonder if he'd already signed off.
Several minutes later, he texted back.

IT'S THE LEAST I CAN DO

21

Nic met me for breakfast the next morning.

"Carnegie escaped," he announced as soon as we'd sat down with our food.

I spit my toast back onto my plate. "I thought you said not to worry about him!"

Nic seemed unruffled. I could tell he was already on his second cup of coffee and had taken some time to prepare his words. "Because I'm legitimately not worried—at least not right now."

"Why not?" I demanded.

"I'm his only alibi."

He slid a tablet across the table. Carnegie's file was displayed on the screen. "Carnegie kept himself—and this entire base— clean. That's why he never involved me in any of this. The United has no idea anything went on up here, then or now. As far as they know, Rott was the center of the action. Mars isn't even on their radar."

I scrolled through Carnegie's file. "But couldn't he turn you in?"

"Of course—at his own expense. If he blows this place up, he destroys his own alibi with it. According to his file, he still works here, and any job transfer would have to be approved by me as his last employer." Nic took the tablet back. "If the officials come snooping into me, they'll find a whole server's worth of intel on him."

"But doesn't he have connections? Couldn't he forge files or alter evidence or something?"

"He *did* have connections—but I think those connections are rotting in the morgue right now."

I gagged.

"Sorry," Nic said, and I think he was being truthful. "What I mean is, I think Thames *was* his connection. Carnegie doesn't have any power on his own. He was, and still is, just an overly ambitious chemical engineer. He doesn't have any clearance with the United. Thames was his master key—the one signing off on reports and issuing blank checks."

"What about Thames's people?"

"Those that are smart will run. We won't have to worry about those that don't."

I shuddered. I hoped Jayde meant what he said about being long gone.

"Your stream told the United exactly where to look. They've probably already razed Thames's office to the ground. They're going to scour those servers—but if Carnegie is as smart as he appears, they won't find anything linking Thames to Mars."

That seemed like a reasonable assumption. Even Jayde hadn't known Thames was involved with Mars, and he worked for him.

Nic stirred a spoon through his coffee, even though I hadn't seen him add any sugar. "He'll be looking for other allies. But the United has no doubt frozen Thames's assets, which means Carnegie is temporarily penniless and homeless. He's going to have to hold his cards close to his chest, and it will take him a long time to rebuild what he had here."

Nic glanced up at me. "He'll be back. I have no doubt of that. But until then, I have the upper hand."

"So why not rat him out first?"

"Because then I'd be throwing myself under the bus. There's millions of bites of data linking Carnegie to me. If I incriminate him, I'll be the first person they investigate." He sighed and ran a hand through his unwashed hair. "I'm going to work on scrubbing the data and distancing myself from him, but it will take time."

"So until then, stalemate."

He nodded.

I rubbed the goosebumps on my arms. Sitting around waiting for one of them to pull the trigger did not sound like my idea of a good time. "So what do we do now?"

"Well, I don't know about you, but I'm going back to work."

I just stared at him.

He gestured at the cafeteria around us. "As far as the United knows, I never left. My file is spotless. Carnegie was careful not to link anything to me, and by some miracle you didn't blow my cover in your impromptu confession. I can, quite literally, pick up where I left off."

I glanced at the people milling around. "But how can you trust these people? How do you know they aren't with Carnegie?"

"There are a few," he admitted. "But they, if anything, have the most incentive to stay quiet."

He leaned back in his chair and eyed me. "You forget, Phil, that you're not the only person here who hates the United. Everyone has a bone to pick. Some, like you, are malcontents. Some want to run experiments that don't have federal approval. Some just don't want to pay taxes."

He nodded at an Asian businessman as he passed our table. The man gave Nic a distracted wave as he continued to chatter into his phone.

"Most of these people don't even know what happened," Nic went on. "Those that do have no reason to tell. Everyone up here has a secret—and they know that if they keep mine, I'll keep theirs."

I gazed at the diverse faces around us. "So what are you going to do now that you're back in business?"

"Keep fortifying my base."

When I shot him an incriminating glare, he put his hands up. "Don't worry, I'm not about to start work on Red Rain."

"And why not?" I countered. It was a genuine question, and every fiber of my being begged him to prove me wrong.

"First of all, it doesn't work on Mars—the atmosphere is too thin. It would only be useful in a large-scale offensive strike against Earth, and thanks to all the damage Carnegie's done, I simply don't have the resources for that kind of wishful thinking right now. Not to mention you also wiped my last database with that virus."

There was a sprinkling of salt in his voice, which I ignored. "And?" I prodded, not satisfied with his explanation.

"And, frankly, I have no desire to start another game of cat-and-mouse with the United. It was fun while it lasted, but I don't want to spend the rest of my life trying to keep the formula out of their hands."

"That's it?" I sputtered. None of those were the reasons I wanted—needed—to hear.

"What do you want me to say, Phil?" he said, too loudly for the ambiance in the room. Several people glanced in our direction. He waited until their eyes drifted elsewhere before continuing.

"Do you want me to apologize? Promise that I'm never going to launch an attack on the United? Swear to never ever do anything that violates your personal moral code?"

Well, at least two of those things would be nice.

"Because I guarantee you that last one *will* happen. The United is still the enemy, and I still intend to fight back."

His eyes found mine. "Look, I don't know how you feel about it, and frankly, I don't care. But revolution has to start somewhere. You said yourself—we can't let them win. We have to fight back. And if you don't want to fight with guns, pick up some other weapon. Write a freaking pamphlet for all I care. But if you want things to change, start changing."

I turned away, churning his words over in my mind.

"But while you're figuring that out, you're welcome to stay here."

I looked back at him. He hit a button on the tablet, then held it out to me again. "There's something you should see."

I took the device and was startled to find my face staring back at me.

It was a personnel file with my picture on it. The photo had been retouched slightly—my hair was lighter, and glasses had been shopped onto my face—but it was definitely me. I squinted at the name on the file.

Andromeda Nolan.

I felt sweat collect on my palms.

"I found it on Thames's computer. Clearly, he had it made for you, and he made himself your legal guardian."

Nolan? Thames Nolan?

The horrible truth drowned me in a rush.

I should have listened to Mrs. Nolan and insisted you stay on Earth.

My husband is well spoken of with the commander; they have agreed on the terms.

When this is all over, I'll do my best to give you a normal life. I promise.

The tablet shook in my hand. I remembered the hair conditioner, Mama's suitcase, the colored pencils—all the little kindnesses that proved he had been watching me for a very long time.

We would have loved you!

"Delete it," I hissed through clenched teeth, afraid that if I opened my mouth, worse things would come out. I threw the tablet on the table, jostling our cups.

Nic watched me carefully. "You might reconsider."

"No," I said without any consideration at all.

"I'm not kidding, Phil. This is a beautiful file."

I glared at him out of the corner of my eye. He tapped the screen. "It has been masterfully forged. It's easy to fake a file—it's not easy to fake one that looks legitimate. This file has everything—perfectly constructed medical and school records that all sync flawlessly with public databases. I did some searching, and I couldn't find anything online that would contradict this file. I even called one of your old schools, and they swore up and down that you were one of their best students. It must have cost him millions to forge this."

"I don't care."

"You should," he shot back. "Your real file is a mess. You're wanted by the highest levels of government, and there's no turning back that clock. But with this—you can walk out of here scot-free. And because you're part of his family, you'll have some special privileges—including some bank accounts, it looks like."

"Won't associating with him get me incriminated?"

"He seems to have thought of that. You're not actually his daughter—you're the daughter of his deceased brother and sister-in-law. It checks out; they had a daughter who would be about your age, and they all died in a car crash, so there's no one to contradict your story. No one's going to think to investigate his dead relatives. He was going to list himself as your legal guardian—but guardianship is easy to change."

I looked up to find him staring at me.

I wretched. "Don't even think about it."

He groaned. "Trust me, this doesn't give me warm-fuzzy feelings either. But I'm your best shot. Your father and brother aren't going to be able to find you based on your old file. At least, if you're associated with me, they have a chance of connecting the dots."

He had a point—a point I couldn't deny. I let my breath out.

"Let me do this for you, and we can call ourselves even on the whole saving-each-other's-lives thing."

In spite of myself, a smile tweaked my lips. "Deal."

He nodded. "All we have to do is get your fingerprints surgically altered just enough. Then we can link the new prints to your file, and you'll be a new person."

"Do you know someone who can do that?"

He rubbed his own fingertips contemplatively. "I can make some calls."

I picked the tablet up and looked at myself again. "Andromeda," I rolled the name over on my tongue.

"Nice to meet you, Andromeda," Nic repeated, then grimaced. "Why can't you pick a name with less than four syllables? I'm calling you Andi."

A laugh escaped my lips.

Andromeda. It didn't sound anything like me.

But maybe that was the point.

I set the tablet back down. "What about my father and brother?"

"Unfortunately, the United is still looking for them. If they're smart, they'll do exactly what you're doing—forge new files."

"Then how am I supposed to find them?" I cried, the hope dying in my words.

"I honestly have no idea."

I slumped in the chair, the energy draining from me as the unanswered questions returned with a vengeance.

"But I'm sure you'll figure something out."

I glanced up. He had gone back to eating and wasn't looking at me.

I straightened. "Well, there's one thing I can try. But I'll need a favor."

One eyebrow twitched to indicate he was listening.

"I need access to Wing 74."

22

The lights in the recording studio flickered on. The place had been swept clean; you couldn't tell there'd been a deadly scuffle in here only a day before. The camera had been polished and straightened, and the folding chair had been set back up in its line of sight.

On the seat was a thin black tube. I walked over and picked it up. It was mascara. Wrapped around it was a piece of masking tape with a microscopic note:

DON'T FORGET TO CONDITION YOUR HAIR -
N

I turned the tube over in my hands, then slid it in my pocket.

A tech I'd only just met had volunteered to run the soundboard. He was in the control booth, spinning around in the chair and salivating over the equipment. "This is a beautiful setup. I wish I could stream my gaming with this."

"You ready in there?" I shot back.

"Let's do it!" He slid up to the desk and tapped a monitor.

I arranged myself in the chair. The viewfinder flickered on. I gazed at my reflection and took a minute to straighten my hair.

"Just give me a signal when you want me to start."

I nodded, closed my eyes, and rehearsed what I was going to say. *Hi. My name is Philadelphia Smyrna.*

The name felt almost foreign now, like it belonged to a different person. Philadelphia Smyrna was the girl who blew up labs, destroyed factories, and sabotaged the United. She resisted. She fought. She was a terrorist. That was the Philadelphia everyone knew.

But, perhaps, she wasn't so foreign to me after all.

I opened my eyes and nodded at the control booth. He gave me a thumbs up and punched a button. The *On Air* sign glowed to life.

I turned to the camera.

"Hey, Dad. It's me, Phil."

TO BE CONTINUED...

PRISONER 120518

RED RAIN #2.5

RACHEL NEWHOUSE
& DAVID HARTUNG

I made it back to my cell just before the door automatically locked, signaling curfew. I turned out the light, slid the cover across the barred window of the door, and sat down at the desk to wait. I'm not sure why the cell had a desk—I hadn't seen a single book or piece of paper on the entire island—but sitting at the empty desk was slightly less dehumanizing than curling up on the weak cot that was too short for my lanky frame.

It wasn't ten minutes later that I heard heavy footsteps and winded breaths enter the corridor. He stopped outside my cell, blocking out the silver of light that crept in under the door.

"Let's talk," he said by way of introduction.

Let's not. I decided to ignore him, mostly just to see what he'd do.

"120518, I know you're in there."

What a Sherlock.

"Open the window."

Nah. I crossed my leg, leaned back in the chair, and waited.

He grunted and cussed. I heard keys rattle, then a swipe of a card in the door. It rejected him with a beep.

I couldn't resist a laugh into the darkness. They hadn't even given him access privileges.

He heard me and swore again. "Open up!"

"You want me to open the door from the inside? That's not how prisons work."

"Do it or I kill you."

"What kind of threat is that? You can't shoot me through the door, unless they gave you one of the good guns, but I don't think you have the clearance."

He mumbled into his communicator.

I lazily stood up and strolled to the door. "How pathetic. You have me in prison on the mainland for months—months!—and hardly say a word to me. Now you swim across the Atlantic to track me down, and you can't even get the door open."

I slid the cover back from the window, revealing an electric pistol aimed at the bars. I was right—it wouldn't have punctured the steel door. It was a child's weapon, really, perfectly suited to the childish man.

I put my hands up. "Please, go ahead. Shoot me. I've been waiting six months for one of you to have the courage."

He spat at me, but the spittle just landed on the handle of his own gun. He grimaced and wiped his hand on his pants.

"What do you want?" I asked. "It's past my bedtime."

He composed himself and put on a smile. "How are you liking Rott, 'Q'?" he slithered, lines clearly rehearsed.

"Don't even try. If you think I'm going to play that song and dance, you're wrong. Just tell me what you want so I can make a show of pondering your offer before slamming this shut in your face." I kept my hand on the window for emphasis.

"You're no fun. At least the Christians put on a good show."

"Then why don't you go back to supervising them, Ambrose? Go back to your cute little concentration camp with a cushy office and a dozen underlings to do your bidding. Go back to watching a bunch of spineless martyrs who don't have the gumption to scale a six-foot wall. Take the easy paycheck, you deserve it."

He was less bothered by that statement than I expected—probably because it was all true, and he didn't mind admitting it. "Maybe when I retire. Right now, though, I've received a better offer."

"Wonderful. I hope your promotion takes you far away from me."

"That is the only downside to this position—it dictates that you and I will be working very closely for the next few months."

"That tells me everything I need to know—I'm not interested, and goodbye."

I slid the window shut. He gave a startled noise I took some pleasure in.

"If you don't..." He swallowed the threat and reinstated his professionalism. "You haven't even heard the employee benefits yet."

"There's nothing you could offer me that would justify those working conditions."

He chuckled. "Really? There's nothing you want? Nothing at all that I could tempt you with? What *do* you want? Money? A state-of-the-art lab? Your own island?"

"I'd consider my own planet. If you offered me Mars, I'd probably play ball, but anything less than that—not interested."

"Your own planet, huh? I think that can be arranged."

"Oh really."

"Well, maybe not a whole planet but—"

"You're lying? How did I know."

"—I think we could spare a moon."

I walked back to the desk. He kept talking, his voice slightly muffled through the door. "We could set you up on a nice, deserted moon. Give you all the supplies you need to build up your own self-sufficient base. Send a few scientists with you to keep you company. We couldn't give you interstellar travel, of course—you've proven you're not trustworthy with it—but we could abandon you to the stars to be the ruler of your own little kingdom."

I stopped, folded my arms, and waited for him to go away.

"That's what you want, isn't it? To be in control. To be free from government regulations and run your own life. To be alone."

I looked to the ceiling. "That last part is spot-on. Can I go to bed now?"

"I have the power. I know the people. I've been authorized to offer you whatever you want, if you'll just do one little project for me."

"And what project is that? What could I possibly offer you that would be worth such a price?"

He savored the moment a beat too long. "Red Rain," he cooed. "You could give us Red Rain, Dr. Nic."

AVAILABLE NOW!

AURELIUS
RED RAIN #3.5
RACHEL NEWHOUSE

My world ended when I saw Philadelphia in the back of the van, cuffed and unconscious.

It was noon when I got the call for two emergency pickups. This was nothing unusual—it was my job, after all. That's why I ran a takeout-only pizza shop. The frequent deliveries were the perfect cover for transporting people who had gotten themselves on the United's bad side.

Cea—or Ceasar, as I knew her—was the one to make the call. I'd been in contact with her off and on over the past few months. She'd been stirring the waters, making a name for herself and figuring out who her friends were, so I knew it was only a matter of time before she needed a pizza.

What I didn't know was that she and I had a history together.

Jayde, our mutual contact, wasn't forthcoming with this information either. Jayde was my first connection with the underground, and we'd worked together enough that we might almost call each other friends. My shop was the closest pickup and dropoff point to the office were Jayde worked. And since Jayde was a guard for a high military official, he was involved in plenty of shenanigans that required pizza delivery.

I hadn't shared a lot of my past with Jayde, but he knew enough to realize that Cea and I had come from the same unassimilated concentration camp. You'd think he would have put two and two together and had the decency to give me a head's up that I might actually *know* the people he was depositing on my doorstep.

Instead, I was wholly unprepared when he opened the back of the van and I saw Philadelphia lying there.

I recognized her instantly, even though she was blindfolded. Her long brown hair pooled around her head like spilled coffee. She wore her favorite outfit—a khaki skirt and gray jacket with leggings and combat boots. It was the same outfit she'd been wearing when I saw her last, the day I left camp for good.

Take their offer while you still can, Phil—take it and run.

The memory of her face—watery eyes begging me to turn around and change my mind—brought with it several other images I was unprepared to handle. My parents, the commander's gun pointed at my chest, Mira, the callous goodbye note taped on our bathroom mirror—everything I had spent the last several months trying to bury came rushing back with all the requisite unwelcome emotions.

You denied Him.

Jayde was unappreciative of my existential crisis. "C'mon, man, we've gotta move!" He'd already uncuffed Cea and helped her down from the van.

I nodded, sweeping the emotions back into the corner of my mind. Jayde knelt next to Philadelphia and removed the cuffs, and I picked her up.

As her dead weight settled in my arms, I saw the dried tears on her face and was slammed with two unsettling realities:

One, she had been through hell.

Two, a *lot* had gone down since I'd left camp.

Jayde helped me get the girls into the bunker, then made himself scarce. The bunker was a concrete cellar under the shop's basement and the one part of the building the government didn't know existed. It was where all my deliveries waited until they could catch a ride somewhere else.

Somehow I had the feeling I couldn't just load Philadelphia on the produce truck and ship her back out of my life.

I laid her out on a blanket in the corner of the bunker, then took care of Cea. I got her a first aid kit and water, and she gave me the rundown while she cleaned and bandaged her own wounds.

The short of it was that Philadelphia's dad, Dr. Smyrna, had been summoned to Mars to work for Cea's brother, Dr. Nic, and gotten tangled up in a weapons plot. Now the United wanted the project finished, and they had been holding Cea and Philadelphia hostage to blackmail the scientists into completing the weapon.

The long of it was that Philadelphia's brother Ephesus, whom we all thought was dead, apparently *wasn't*, and the project was a world-ending superweapon called "Red Rain," and Philadelphia had blown up a lab and turned Nic over to the authorities, and now the United wanted the weapon for themselves, and Jayde's boss, Director Thames Nolan, was overseeing the project.

Luckily for all involved, Cea knew how to order pizza.

None of this really surprised me, except maybe the part about Ephesus coming back to life and definitely the part about Philadelphia blowing up a lab by herself.

I watched her sleep from across the room and wondered if she was the same girl I had left behind.

AVAILABLE NOW!

WANT EXCLUSIVE BONUS SCENES?

Get access to **exclusive bonus scenes** for this series by becoming a Patron! For as little as $1 a month, you'll receive prerelease copies of all my books with bonus material not available anywhere else. Plus, you can get signed paperbacks, collector's edition hardbacks, and merch, or read my WIP as I write it!

Become a Patron at:
patreon.com/rachelnewhouse

Or sign up for my newsletter and be the first to hear about new releases—plus get sneak peeks of upcoming books, cover art, and more!

Sign up at:
rachelnewhouse.com/subscribe

DID YOU LOVE THIS BOOK?

Please consider leaving a review on Amazon or Goodreads! It's one of the most important things you can do to support an indie author. Thank you!

HI FROM RACHEL

Rachel Newhouse is an author, wife, secretary, and Sunday school teacher from Kansas City, Missouri. Her obsessions are sci-fi, dystopian, and kid lit. When she's not writing, she's cooking Asian food, growing chilis that are too spicy to eat, and watching wildly age-inappropriate shows like *My Little Pony* and *Gravity Falls* with her husband, Joe. She also really likes glitter. You've been warned.

Connect with Rachel:
bio.site/rachelnewhouse